THE GOBLIN'S VALENTINE

AN EQUILOAM ROMAQNCE

MONA HOWELL

Cover Designer: MelMul

Editor: Sangeet Pandey

Copy Editor: Heartfelt Editing

Sensitivity Reader: Shannon Clark

Author Photo: Emily Winnie Photography

CONTENT WARNING

The Goblin's Valentine is an adult interspecies fantasy romance short story. It contains adult themes and explicit content, including but not limited to: external stimulation, prey vs. predator arousal and copulation, voyeurism, earthen materials, and external sexual stimulation via material contact. Some content may not be suitable for readers with sensitivities to: the idea of interspecies coupling, extensively descriptive sexual situations, prejudice or racist themes (fantasy), the existence of magic, or those who may take issue with predatory arousal and descriptions of violent ideology.

For Heather

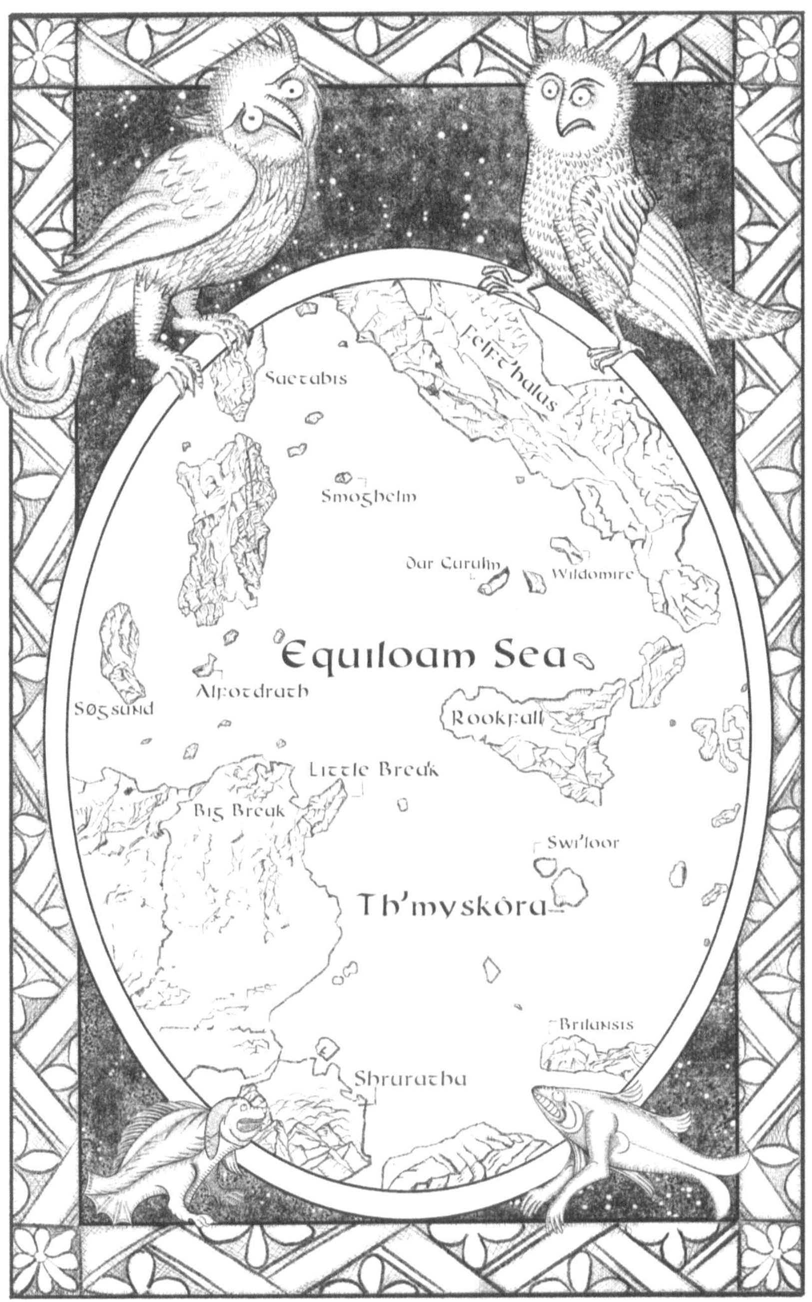

Saetabis
Felr'thalas
Smoghelm
Oar Curulm
Wildomire
Equiloam Sea
Alr̥otdrath
Søgsund
Rookfall
Little Break
Big Break
Swi'loor
Th'myskóra
Brilansis
Shruratha

CHAPTER I

DITHER

Dither pulled her heavy woolen cloak tight around her shoulders, bracing against the freezing winter rain. She squeezed between two massive granite stones, wriggling her tiny shoulders and digging her bare toes into the mud. The little goblin shoved with all the might in her tiny body, desperate to penetrate the slick hole in the outer wall of the ancient troll ruins. On the other side was an architectural marvel: a series of mangled hexagonal structures, all touching, built on sacred troll geometry long ago, now in varying stages of decay.

"Jack . . ." she grunted. "Valentine . . ." She was through to her slight hips now. Dither pressed her nimble green fingers against the wall and gave one final shove. " . . . must be satisfied!"

She popped through the hole and splashed face-first into an ice-cold puddle. Mud dripped from her long, pointed ears, and she plucked an earthworm from her caul.

"This is no time for a snack," the little goblin said, getting to her feet and wringing out her skirts. "You've got a mission to complete."

The wreckage of the troll Stronghold contained the oldest structures anywhere on the island of Th'myskôra, the stone corpse of a once-great city. Dither darted through the predawn gloom from one massive, ruined structure to another, crawling over and under cracked stone blocks, scraping her shins on the crumbling edges of what used to be homes and shops and armories.

"It's here," she muttered. "I can feel it."

Dither closed her eyes and placed her hands over her chest, letting the rain caress her face, feeling the wet earth beneath her moss-lined feet.

"Oh, Jack Valentine, you great sprite, you master of japes, lead me to the treasure so that I might enact revelry in your honor."

Dither felt a pang in her chest, and her eyes snapped open. "There!" she squeaked as the flattened remains of the troll blacksmith came into view in the distance.

She ran across the Stronghold, splashing through the rain and leaping over boulders, her oversized bell sleeves fluttering like standards in the wind.

This was the spot; it had to be. Dither sank to her knees, digging frantically through the mud until her willowy arms were submerged past the elbow. Would it really still be here after these many hundreds of years?

Yes! Buried in a corner and wrapped in disintegrating shrew leather was a large wooden box. She reached deep into the pit and tugged at the thing, jerking it back and forth in an effort to free it from hundreds of years of neglect . . . and mud. She wrestled it out, set the box down on a flat boulder, and ran her fingers over its still-intact copper hinges. The lock was brittle and caked with rust. Dither grabbed a slippery rock and bashed it apart with one blow. She held her breath and carefully opened the box.

Inside were thirty-eight perfect troll keys, each one shaped by hand, unique to the world.

Dither grabbed a key, admiring the craftsmanship, kissing it, and holding it to her breast.

"Perfect," she squeaked. "You're going to be so shiny once I'm done with you!" Grinning, she stowed the key back in its box with the others and tucked the treasure under her cloak, ready to make her escape.

WHAM!

Something huge and heavy and fast knocked Dither to the ground. She struggled to free herself, her face buried in the mud. Sharp talons pinning her to the earth.

"Please," she coughed out a mouthful of mud. "Please, let me go."

The hot, threatening presence pressed closer.

"I, um . . . I didn't know the Stronghold was off-limits?" Adrenaline coursed through her tiny body.

The thing on top of her leaned in, brushing its soft feathers against her cheek. Fear prickled the back of Dither's neck, and her heart raced.

"Fine!" she cried. "I *did* know! I knew, and I'm very sorry. Now let me up!"

"Dither?" said a familiar voice. "Dither Weaselsnout, is that you?"

A barely-audible rustling of feathers whispered past Dither's ears as the thing climbed off, and she scrambled to her feet. There, standing in the unrelenting rain, was the towering form of Aldonas, the strix. Dither looked from his taloned feet up to his leathery black legs, then powerful, muscular thighs covered in a thick layer of blood-red feathers. Finally, she stood straight up and found herself face-to-face with Aldonas' copper cock. It was erect, and even in the near-dark of the early morning, she saw it glint and shimmer as rivulets of ice-cold rainwater ran down to its base and dripped in an unrelenting stream onto his feathers.

"So *shiny*," she muttered, eyes wide, mouth watering.

"Good morning," the strix said, his beak gritted.

"Aldonas!" She'd almost forgotten there was a whole owlman attached to that beautiful copper member. Dither forced her gaze up to his large, flat avian face. "You look . . . *different*. Are you redder than normal?"

"W-what?" he stammered, clicking his curved beak. "No, you just . . . no one was supposed to see me tonight."

"Your feathers are *definitely* redder than usual," Dither blathered. "Your breast feathers are white, like normal, but all your other feathers are *blood* red!"

Aldonas took a couple of clumsy steps backward, but Dither's appraisal continued.

"Your eyes!" she gasped. "They're completely yellow! What happened to your pupils? Not that I spend a lot of time thinking about your eyes or anything . . . although I *have* seen them this way one other time, when you were making a crazed sort of hungry face, like you are right now—"

"My pupils recede when hunting," he sighed, turning his large, round head from one side to the other.

"Hunting? Is *that* why you're naked?" Dither's eyes drifted back down to his gleaming cock. "Didn't want to get blood all over your clothes, huh?"

Aldonas folded his massive wings closed, shielding his body from Dither's view.

"And your shiny, metal dick is all the way out of its little owl pouch! That *can't* help you fly faster." She tapped her chin thoughtfully. "Just think of the drag!"

Aldonas shifted his weight in the mud and cleared his throat. Dither barreled on, tripping over her words and speaking at breakneck speed.

"Oh!" She smacked herself on the forehead. "I shouldn't have said anything. I always talk too much when I'm nervous. It's a terrible habit, but why should I be nervous? It's not like I haven't seen you naked before. Of course, that was a year and a half ago. When we had sex. In the live oak trees outside of the Academy. Remember?"

Aldonas' beak fell open.

"Of course you remember . . . It was sex. But then, you've barely spoken to me since, so maybe it was sex you'd rather not remember." Even in the pouring rain, Dither could feel the heat creeping through her body and spreading to her cunt; she would have loved another chance at the shining metal rod.

"But I've said too much — *much* too much. Tell me about . . . *yourself*. Do you hunt nude often?" She leaned one elbow against a slippery granite block, hoping desperately to look nonchalant. "Where do you get a permit for that kind of thing?"

Dither's eyes kept settling straight ahead at Aldonas' crotch; she could just barely see it glinting between his feathers. "Does the . . . um . . . copper penis aid at all in the, um . . . killing process? I suppose you could use it as a lure; it's so shiny . . . It sure would lure me. I guess it already *did* lure me . . . to the sex that we had. Anyway . . . what sort of prey were you hoping to find out here in these abandoned ruins, anyway?"

Aldonas blinked and shook his head. His pupils slowly reappeared. "My penis . . ." he said, "emerges in the presence of certain . . . stimuli. It does not normally play a role in the hunt."

"Am *I* the stimuli?" Dither squeaked and slapped both hands over her mouth.

"Speaking of ruins." His feathers bristled. "The Stronghold is largely considered off-limits. What are *you* doing out here in the rain?"

"Me?" Dither stepped casually in front of her wooden box. "I was just . . . going for an early-morning walk . . ."

"And you wouldn't be trying to remove anything from a historical site without council approval, would you?"

"What? Me? Never!" She bent down slowly and slid the box under her arm.

"Dither," Aldonas said, tapping his scaly foot in the mud, "what's under your cloak?"

"Nothing!" she squeaked. "Gotta go!" Dither backed quickly out of the blacksmith's and scrambled towards the wall.

"Don't run from me, Dither. Please!" As he spoke, Aldonas' voice cracked into a wild, animalistic screech.

"I wasn't *going* to run from you," she said, hiking up her skirts. "But I am now!"

"Bring back that box!" Aldonas called through the storm as Dither sprinted back to the hole in the wall.

Dither didn't dare look over her shoulder as she skidded through puddle after puddle, nearing the wall.

Aldonas was lumbering after her, much slower and clumsier on his feet than he was in the air.

"Stop running!" he shouted. "Please!"

"You know," Dither panted, "you're coming off very judgy for a guy stumbling through the mud with his cock out." She crouched behind a fallen tree — the last cover between her and the wall.

"Alright, Dither, you can make it," she muttered and put her head down, racing as fast as her little legs could carry her.

Aldonas was hot on her heels, for some reason still running.

I can beat him, as long as he doesn't fly. I can beat him.

The wall was only feet away when a terrible screech tore through the air.

Adrenaline surged through Dither at the sound, and she hurled herself across the final stretch. She slid the box through the hole and jumped, scrabbling at the dripping granite. A flash of crimson flew overhead.

"Frogs!" She cursed and jumped again, this time catching hold of a divot in the rock.

Aldonas made another pass. His screeching ceased as soon

as he took to the sky. When he was flying, Aldonas was silent, elegant — an efficient killing machine.

Dither pulled herself through the hole, back safely in the Eldrich Forest. No titan could enter an enchanted forest unaccompanied, not even a crazed strix.

Dither climbed up a rock and pressed her face against the hole. "Bye, Aldonas," she called cheerily. "I'll see you at work!"

CHAPTER 2

ALDONAS

"Finally, class," Aldonas said, sinking the razor-sharp tip of his beak into the fleshy part of his wing. Three drops of blood splashed into the abalone shell on his desk. "The practitioner must add the essence of his own life to the mixture, for without sacrifice, nothing of value can be attained."

He pretended not to notice the shocked gasps and looks of revulsion on the faces around the lecture hall. If he were being honest, Aldonas delighted in disabusing students of the notion that the practice of the sacred arts was some kind of glittering wish-casting.

"Now," he picked up a small pestle fashioned from a narwhal tooth and crushed the ingredients together. It was difficult, as always, to control the fine implements with the specialized feathers at the ends of his enormous wings, but Aldonas wasn't the kind of person to let a little thing like lacking fingers get in his way.

When he'd first arrived on Th'myskôra as a fresh-faced student, Aldonas had spent countless hours locked away in his room, forcing his awkward body to do what everyone said it would never be capable of. Now he was a competent professor, the epitome of self-control. None of the students watching his demonstration today would ever guess how much effort Aldonas was employing — and that was exactly according to plan.

"Once the paste is created," he said, lifting the abalone bowl to show the spell's consistency, "the practitioner must focus his attention on his desire. The greater the focus, and the stronger the desire, the more successful the casting."

"Pay attention, Grover," a siren muttered, elbowing his friend in the ribs. "Maybe you'll get a date to the Valentine's Feast!"

"What was that, Mr. Quaff?" Aldonas asked, turning his head nearly completely around and fixing his menacing yellow eyes on the boys. The lecture hall was raked and circular, with Aldonas' desk situated at the lowest point in the center of the room. Apparently, the mischievous youths thought they could escape their professor's attention by sitting in the top row, behind his back. Not so.

"N-nothing, professor," stammered Kreston Quaff the siren. "We were just having some fun — you know, because the festival is coming up so soon."

"There's always a festival coming up on Th'myskôra," Aldonas snapped. "Is that an excuse to talk during my lecture?"

"No, professor," said Mr. Quaff, blushing.

"Mr. Gribble." Aldonas turned his attention to the other boy. "*Could* you use this low stone spell to obtain a date?"

The class giggled. Grover Gribble, the were-vole, squirmed in his seat.

"Probably not."

"And why not, Mr. Gribble?"

"Because women are big?"

A torrent of laughter erupted in the study hall. Grover slid down in his chair.

"Why wouldn't you be able to attract a big woman with this spell?"

"The . . . um . . . low stone spell is best applied to the acquisition of trinkets or other small items for which the user has a very strong desire? It's, um . . . just not that powerful a spell?"

"Very good, Mr. Gribble." Aldonas turned his attention back to the class at large and resumed the demonstration. "Now, hold very firmly to your desire as you spread the mixture across your infraclavicular and recite the following: *Oh, little thing, tiny joy, come into my life. 'Tis long that I have yearned for you to turn my darkness bright.*"

A hush fell over the room as all fifty-two students watched

their professor hungrily, anticipating the appearance of some unknown oddity on his desk.

"It takes a few days to work," Aldonas announced, large eyes crinkling. "When we next meet, you should all be prepared to execute your own low stone spell, so think long and hard about what you want to conjure."

The class grumbled, and wooden chair legs scraped against the polished stone floor as students began shoving books and parchment into their satchels.

"Remember," Aldonas called over the din, "the more you want it, the stronger your spell will be."

"Speaking of strong spells," a familiar voice squeaked at his elbow. "I don't suppose I could get one of those feathers for a love potion, could I?"

"Dither!" Aldonas nearly jumped out of his britches when he noticed the tiny goblin caressing one of his long, brown tail feathers. "I didn't hear you come in."

"Soft feet." She tugged one ankle in the air to show him the thick pad of moss growing on the underside of her foot. "They're great for sneaking into all kinds of places you shouldn't be . . ."

"Yes, yes, very good," Aldonas said, rearranging the papers on his desk as the last of his students shuffled out the door. If his face weren't covered in feathers, they would have seen him blushing at the tantalizing sight of her bare ankle. "What — ahem — brings you here today, Miss Weaselsnout?"

"*Miss* Weaselsnout?" Dither's large eyes began to water, and her lower lip quivered ever so slightly. Most people would have missed the subtle shift, but Aldonas' keen strix senses were finely attuned to his prey. "That's awfully formal," she muttered before turning her slight, angular green face back up to him. "I'm here to record your acquisition requests for next week."

Dither rummaged through her small wooden push cart and retrieved a piece of parchment and a quill. When she stood, her slightly too-large gown fell to one side, exposing her delicately sculpted shoulder. Aldonas' eyes followed the low, sweeping neckline of the rough blue woolen dress, down her shoulder and across her chest, where he could just barely make out the tops of her small, pert breasts. He dragged his eyes slowly up past her clavicle, to her delicate neck and the hot, sticky ambrosia pulsing through it. Dither parted her full, green lips and slid the tip of her pink tongue out to wet the tip of her quill.

Aldonas' heartbeat rang in his ears, driving out all other sounds. He felt the copper rod stir inside its feather-lined pouch, threatening escape. The tip of his culmen, the rounded bridge of his beak, lengthened into a razor-sharp point as he stared, transfixed. His vision focused on her as everything in his periphery faded into a hazy mist of vague shapes.

" . . . so that's fifty-two ounces of barley flour, fifty-two dried woundwarts, and fifty-two green tiger beetles?" Dither asked. The scraping of her quill across parchment broke through his daze. "Do you want extras of anything? The beetles tend to wander off."

"Where is Bronthilda?" Aldonas asked, blinking himself back into the present.

"What?"

"Bronthilda. She's been getting my supplies for the last three terms. Where is she?"

"Oh, sorry." The tips of Dither's long, pointed green ears burned red. "She's having her baby. I'm covering the third floor for her for the rest of the term."

"Of course, yes. She has seemed rather pregnant lately."

"So . . . I'll just put you down for fifty-five of the beetles, then, if there's nothing else..." Dither turned to wheel her little cart out of the room.

"Wait!" Aldonas flung himself in her path. "You say you'll be outfitting all of my classes for the next four months?"

"Well, yeah . . ." Dither said, maneuvering around him. "It's February now; classes end in June, that's . . ." — she counted on her fingers — "four months!"

"No! That is — I wouldn't want you to worry yourself on my account." His gape watered. Aldonas could practically taste her sweet blood dribbling down his throat. "I'll just get them myself."

"You most certainly will not!" Dither balled her tiny fists and planted them on her hips.
"Only trained personnel are allowed in the storeroom!"

As she stared indignantly up at him, her breasts heaving, her prominent nostrils flaring, Aldonas' desire swelled. Memories of their dalliance in the live oaks two summers ago flooded his mind. The image of Dither's face, twisted with ecstasy; the sounds of her tiny, whimpered moans; the smell of desire spilling out of her and coating his copper cock, all echoed through his mind. Now that he'd felt her lithe body crushed to the earth under his talons, now that he'd allowed himself to pursue her through the early morning gloom, his need was maddening.

"I'll be in and out!" Aldonas shouted as he shoved past Dither and charged down the hallway. "It won't take a moment."

The little goblin abandoned her cart and scurried after him. "Hey," she hissed, "what part of 'not allowed' do you not understand?"

Aldonas' legs were twice as long as Dither's, but the four curved talons tipping each foot made walking quickly across slick marble floors nearly impossible. She easily kept pace with him, her shrill condemnations drawing the attention of staff and students alike.

"Everything alright out here?" asked Professor Oloborous, blinking his eight beady black eyes in succession.

"Yes, yes," Aldonas said. "We're just discussing me accessing the Academy storeroom." His pace quickened, and so did his heart rate. Aldonas' gait became increasingly unsightly as his talons scraped and slid along the floor. If he flew, he could overtake her easily — but then he'd transform again into a bloodthirsty beast. "Surely you can make an exception for me... since we're old friends?"

"Old friends?" That stopped Dither in her tracks, and Aldonas was able to get a few feet closer to the service stairwell. "I didn't realize that twenty minutes of sex followed by six months of you *ignoring* me qualified us as 'old friends.'"

Well, that will certainly give everyone something to gossip about. Aldonas kept charging toward the stairwell as nosy students and staff poked their heads into the hallway. *One thing they* won't *be able to say is that I disemboweled the storage goblin.*

Aldonas reached the door to the service stairs — a dusty, narrow wooden staircase not meant for general use, illuminated by only the smallest occasional window. Wrapping his feathers around the iron pull, he yanked the door open. "Perhaps you'd consider it a professional courtesy, then?" he asked, launching down the narrow wooden stairs. He could feel her heat at his back, spreading through his body, calling the blood-red pigment into his feathers.

"Professional?" Dither rushed down the cramped stairwell, squirming against Aldonas, invading his senses with her soft, warm little body. How easily would his talons rip through her flesh? How much resistance would her slick cunt offer as he pumped his metal cock inside it?

"A *professional* would submit an acquisition request like every other professor and let me do my job," she squeaked.

They reached the second-story landing, a worn wooden

platform just wide enough for Dither to push past. Aldonas pursued her again down the dimly-lit staircase, away from the prying eyes of anyone who might intercede.

"I have serious doubts as to whether you'll meet the high standard Bronthilda set."

The goblin gasped and stopped, stunned for a moment on the stairs.

Good. I can't chase her if she isn't running.

"I happen to be excellent at my job," Dither protested, pulling fruitlessly at the back of his tunic as he pushed past her. "If you would wait for your request to be processed, you would see that."

They reached the first-story landing. From here on, there would be no more windows to provide dim light, no more subtle stream of fresh air. The little goblin's scent was all around him, wet earth and almond oil, his copper cock bucked in response.

Her tiny body scrambled deeper and deeper into the earth, illuminated only by flickering candles. The darker the stairwell became, the sharper his vision, the more acute his thirst. Finally, they reached the basement landing. Dither raced to a large wooden door and turned to face him, placing her tiny hands firmly on her slim hips.

"Don't you dare come into this room!" she threatened.

"I'm sorry," Aldonas said as self-control abandoned him.

He wrapped his massive wings around Dither and crashed through the door. Inside the storeroom, he crouched over her limp body, digging his terrible talons into the yielding wood planks beneath them. Aldonas wasn't sure if he would feast on her entrails or ravage her sex, but either way, she was entirely at his mercy.

CHAPTER 3

DITHER

"Floatin' frogs!" Dither blinked herself back to consciousness. Her vision was blurry, and the back of her head stung. Aldonas hunched over her, massive wings spread. His feathers were blood red and his large pupils had disappeared, leaving haunting yellow orbs that gleamed down at her in the dim candlelight.

"I wanted your attention, but this is a bit much," she said weakly.

Aldonas seemed to come to his senses. He staggered backward, stumbling and bumping into a large wooden card catalogue, crashing into carefully stacked specimen cases, and kicking over piles of books. He blinked hard and shook his head, muttering something Dither couldn't make out.

She got to her feet and rushed over to her desk, rummaging through its drawers for a small bundle wrapped in cotton. She took half its contents and mixed them in a tankard of water.

"Get out of here!" Aldonas shrieked. "Escape while you still can!"

"*You* get out of here," she said, sitting cross-legged on her desk and taking a big gulp from her tankard. "This is *my* storeroom!" She watched as the strix's breathing became more regular and his movements less erratic. Finally, he sank to the floor, cradling his head in his wings.

"That's better," Dither said, draining the last of her solution. "Now, do you mind telling me what in three hells is going on?"

When Aldonas looked up at her, his beak and eyes were back to normal. "I'm sorry, I ..." He turned his head two hundred seventy degrees from left to right, taking in the enormity of the storeroom. "I'm sorry I ever thought I'd be able to find my way around in this place."

"That's right!" Dither said, hopping off her desk with a satisfied little grunt. "There are over three hundred thousand items in this storeroom alone."

She walked over to Aldonas with the remaining dried herb. "Open your mouth." He obeyed, and Dither popped it past his beak. "Well, now that you've seen it, you can go back up to the third floor and act normal." She turned away, getting to work righting the disheveled piles of books left in his wake.

"I don't know if I can." Aldonas struggled to his feet and joined her in cleaning up the mess. "What did I just eat, by the way?"

"Willowbark, for the headache I assume you have — bog knows I do!"

"Right," he said, rubbing the back of his head. "Dither . . . how much do you know about strixes?"

"Not much," she admitted. "I always assumed you were giant owls. Like birdmen?"

Aldonas sighed. "A strix is something much worse . . ."

"Oh?" Dither bit her lip, the memory of their hurried indiscretion flashing across her mind. She'd only begun to slide her eager cunt down his inflexible metal shaft when they'd been interrupted.

"I've worked my whole life to control my urges," he said, pacing across the room, "to be the master of my own actions. But when I'm around you, Dither . . . I . . ." He hesitated. "I become a monster."

Dither's heart sank. "I get it — you don't like me."

"It's not that, Dither. I just can't . . ." Aldonas hung his head.

"You can't stand to be around me. I know. That's what you always say, right after I catch you following me around."

"I can't see you running . . . in and out of my classroom every day."

Dither's lip trembled. How could she have been so stupid to

think Aldonas would ever want to be with someone like her? Why did she always let him get her hopes up?

"Be that as it may," she huffed, "it would be impossible for you to locate your own supplies."

The walls were twenty feet high and covered with neatly organized potions, spells, trinkets, and tomes. The subterranean catacombs stretched on, packed with endless rows of massive wooden shelves housing magical items.

"No, I don't suppose I could," Aldonas said, swiveling his large flat face around. "Perhaps I'd better take a leave of absence, just until Bronthilda is back at work . . ."

"Don't be silly," Dither said, patting him on the wing, foolishly watching his face for signs of the beast who'd chased her down the stairwell. She let her hand linger, and Aldonas' pupils did, indeed, begin to fade away. Dither's heart danced in her tiny chest. "If there's one thing goblins are known for, it's finding things — and that includes solutions."

"Dither, I appreciate your desire to help, but—"

Dither held up her tiny hand, silencing him. "Write me a list."

"I'm sorry?"

"At the end of the week, write a list and pin it to the outside of your door. I'll collect it after you leave on Friday and leave you a supply cart on Monday morning. You'll never have to see me again."

"Oh." Aldonas ran one wing over the back of his head. "I can't believe I didn't think of that. It's so easy."

"Most problems are pretty easy, once you stop thinking you have to do everything yourself."

"Yeah . . . well, that . . . thank you." Aldonas turned to leave, then stopped at Dither's desk. "This box . . ."

"Oh, no!" she wailed, running over and clutching the box to her chest.

"This is what you took from the Stronghold this morning, isn't it?"

"I need them! You don't understand — it takes the council *ages* to approve everything. I'd never have them in time for the Valentine's Feast!"

Aldonas' eyes flashed yellow once more, but as Dither slowly put the box back down on her desk and backed away, his features returned to normal. He opened the box and revealed the collection of ancient, tarnished keys.

"Troll-make?" he asked, lifting one key from the box and examining it. "You know any artifact preceding The War must be analyzed by the Committee for Cultural Preservation. Technically, I should turn these in."

"And technically, *I* should report you. Last I checked, tackling coworkers was frowned upon."

"Well played." Aldonas returned the key to the box. "Why do you want a bunch of keys with no locks anyway?"

"Oh," Dither chuckled. "I've had the locks for years. I've been looking for their keys since I moved to the island. Now that I have them, I'll finally be able to satisfy the spirit of Jack Valentine!"

Aldonas quirked his head. "You don't really believe in Jack Valentine, do you? I thought that was just a children's fairytale."

"Jack Valentine is very real," Dither said firmly, "and when I trick all those couples into bonding for life, he will be well pleased with me!"

"You can't *make* people fall in love."

"Of course you can!" Dither bounced excitedly on her toes, thrilled, as always, to explain the teachings of Jack Valentine. "All you have to do is find people who are compatible and get them together at the sacred hour of sunset on Valentine's Day. Then *they* just have to interact with a cursed object — in this case, the locks and keys — and Jack Valentine takes care of the rest!"

"That seems less than ethical," said Aldonas. "What about attraction? What about choice?"

"Love potion helps with that," said Dither, eying his tail feathers.

"Love potions made from strix feathers are especially

potent," Aldonas said curtly. "It's not a power that can be entrusted to just anybody." As he spoke, Aldonas turned ever so slightly, shielding his tail feathers from Dither's nimble fingers.

"Don't worry, I'm not going to steal them," Dither murmured. "Unless you give me no other choice . . ."

"Yes. Well . . ." Aldonas' tail twitched. "Good luck with your, um, religious observance."

"Thank you." Dither smiled and turned to lift a pile of newly-acquired dragon scales. They'd already been catalogued; she just had to find a cozy spot for them on the right shelf. When she straightened, little arms loaded with heavy, glistening disks, she felt the unmistakable heat of Aldonas at her back.

"Is there something else I can help you with?"

"No. Thank you."

Dither tightened her arms around the large, grooved scales and walked down the long, narrow path between rows of shelves. As she went, she continued to hear the sound of hard talons scraping against the wooden floor.

Aldonas was following her.

"You're doing it again," she groaned. "That thing where you say you don't want to be around me and then you follow me around."

"Sorry," Aldonas muttered. "I'm trying to leave."

"Well, try a little harder. I've got work to do." Dither spun around to face him. His eyes shone yellow in the dim basement light, just as they had when he'd chased her through the Stronghold. Just as they had when he'd yanked her dress off over her head during that hurried indiscretion. Dither's mouth watered. She thought of him tackling her, naked in the mud. She longed to feel his soft feathers caress her bare skin.

He slid a wing across her arm, and squonkbumps sprang up in response. "Maybe I could help you put these away?"

"No. Thank you." Dither forced herself to take a step back, abandoning the warmth of his feathers. "If we're never going to see each other again, we should probably start now."

"You're right. Of course."

Dither turned again, passing rows of shelves, moving from one interconnected room to the next.

Aldonas followed her.

This was how it always was between them. When Dither had first come to the Academy, she'd been immediately smitten by the beautiful, massive strix — his broad chest straining against his tunic; muscular, scaled calves peeking out beneath fine silk britches. But when she tried to introduce herself, he ran off.

Aldonas kept her at wing's length, always stopping her from confessing her attraction, but never letting her get too far out of his sight. If Dither hadn't known better, she might have thought he was deliberately egging her crush on.

Dither turned left, toward the magical dermis room. "What you're doing right now is the opposite of leaving," she said without looking at him.

"Sorry," Aldonas creaked. Every time he spoke, his voice grew more screech-like.

In all the months he'd been playing mind games with her, she'd never heard him apologize; of course, she'd never been bold enough to call him out before, either.

She stepped on the bottom rung of the ladder leaning against the wall of cursed keratin and started climbing slowly. Aldonas groaned, and she knew he was watching her perky, round ass shift and bulge under her skirts.

Dither, it doesn't matter how beautiful he is. It doesn't matter how shiny his cock is. You can't keep pining over him. Aldonas doesn't want you back — not the way you want him. This has got to stop.

"You're still in my storeroom," she said, pausing with her ass positioned exactly at his eye level.

"I . . ." Aldonas' voice was strained and animalistic. "I want you."

Dither reached up, carefully placing the scales on the shelf one at a time, savoring the excited clicking of Aldonas' beak and the guttural chirps that escaped him as she stretched and swayed on her perch.

"Do you?" she asked, turning carefully on the ladder to observe him. Aldonas stood several feet away, feathers darkened, eyes half-wild. "Or do you never want to see me again?"

"I want you, Dither!" he crowed.

To hells with it! What's a goblin if not beholden to her chaotic desires?

"Come over here," Dither commanded.

Aldonas took a couple of shaky steps forward and Dither thrilled — Aldonas the strix was obeying *her* commands. His large, unblinking eyes fixed on her. Dither's nipples tightened against her rough cotton bindings.

"Closer," she instructed, thrilled by the authority in her own voice.

Aldonas braced himself against the shelf, one wing on either side of Dither's tiny, trembling body. She leaned down and brushed her cheek against his incredibly soft feathers. "How are you feeling?" she asked him.

"Embarrassed," Aldonas said, "and aroused . . ."

Embarrassed that he wants me.

"Let's just get this out of our systems," Dither said, shaking her head. "Then will you leave?

"Yes," Aldonas croaked.

"Fine. You owe me an orgasm anyway." Dither placed her hands carefully on Aldonas' shoulders. "I'd like to kiss you; would *that* be alright?"

"Yes."

Dither bent slowly toward the massive strix, her mouth watering.

For as long as she'd known Aldonas, Dither had longed for him. When they'd finally shared a few minutes of rushed, clumsy lovemaking two summers ago, she was sure their romance would finally begin.

How do you stop wanting a man who will never want you back?

She dragged the side of her nose along Aldonas' beak. His head fell forward ever so slightly, and she breathed in his scent. They were about to make love again — only this time she had no delusions about his feelings for her.

"I want you, Dither," he groaned. "Please."

She rested her forehead against Aldonas', sliding her fingers through his feathers and cupping his wide, flat face in her hands.

There's nothing wrong with having a little casual sex. That's all this was ever going to be. Super casual sex.

Dither could feel her heart pounding in her chest. She breathed deeply, slowly, attempting to control it. In a few moments, she'd feel his cold, copper cock sliding into her again.

Dither worked her hands through Aldonas' feathers to the back of his head. She balled her fists and pulled.

Aldonas moaned and trembled, his beak growing longer with each exhalation.

Dither tilted her head. She parted her lips and pressed them to the side of his beak.

CHAPTER 4
ALDONAS

eed! Fuck! Devour!

Hunger surged through Aldonas' body. He felt his beak growing, ripping through his face to present itself at its full, terrible length. His vision narrowed, and the room in which he had been standing moments ago dissolved into a formless mist the moment the goblin's soft pout touched his beak.

"Take off your tunic," her melodic voice commanded, barely audible through the din of their pounding hearts.

"Scraw!" Aldonas didn't want to take his wings off her for a second — *she could escape!*

"You have to get undressed if we're going to have sex," said the goblin.

Aldonas trilled. He removed his tunic, britches, and small-clothes as quickly as he could, never taking his piercing gaze off the tiny, squirming goblin.

"Shiiinyyyyy," the goblin said, looking down at his copper cock, and Aldonas puffed with pride.

Shiny cock. Best cock.

He clacked his beak open and closed, emitting a series of excited chirps. Aldonas lunged at the goblin, catching hold of the hem of her dress and tugging at it with his beak.

"Hey!" the goblin cried. "Restrain your shrews! I'll take off my own clothes, if you don't mind."

Aldonas took half a step back and watched excitedly, quirking his head from one side to the other as she wriggled out of her dress. The heavy garment hit the floor, but there were still more layers. His cock thrummed and lurched impatiently. A second, lighter dress appeared, and the goblin quickly removed and tossed it aside too. Below that, thin strips of linen were wrapped many times around her breasts. Aldonas wanted to tear them off her, but he stayed in his place, following instructions.

The goblin's shoulders were bare. Her thin arms and expert fingers worked quickly to untie the strips, letting each one float gently to the floor. Finally, her breasts were free. Aldonas saw her bright pink nipples standing in contrast to perky green breasts, and his copper cock began to hum, a high-pitched metallic vibration that filled his ears and made him pounce on her again.

"Eat!" His talons dug into the wooden shelves against

which her ladder leaned. Shards of wood splintered, scratching the leathery skin of his feet.

Aldonas chomped down on Dither's woolen caul, tossing it aside and revealing a tangle of swampy green hair perfumed with almond oil. He tugged her head with his beak, thrusting his pelvis at her. He screeched and humped in the air.

"Not. Yet," the goblin said firmly, and he hopped back onto the floor, clicking his beak impatiently as he stared at her beautiful crotch. Aldonas could hear the blood pounding through her sex, swelling her clit for him.

"That's better," said Dither, and she slid off her smallclothes, exposing a tuft of lush green pubic hair that Aldonas very much wanted to bite.

He cried and chittered and scratched at the floor, but didn't charge at her, not even when the little goblin sat on the ladder rung exactly opposite his mouth and spread her legs, revealing her bright pink entrance.

"Alright," she finally said. "I want you to walk over here, very slowly."

Aldonas obeyed, his pulse racing, his large, round eyes fixed on her glistening pussy.

"I want you to lick it," the goblin said, grinning. "Can you handle that?"

Aldonas hooted wildly, flapping his wings and bobbing his head. "Yes!" he chittered, thrusting his face toward his meal.

"Gently!" The goblin placed a tiny palm on his forehead and guided him slowly.

Aldonas pressed his beak against her clit. The goblin let out a satisfied moan, and Aldonas' copper cock pinged again. He slid his culmen up and down her sex, coating it in her slick and earning a torrent of squeaks and moans. Finally, she pulled his head closer and placed her little feet on his shoulders, guiding him toward her pleasure.

Aldonas opened his mouth, letting his long, red tongue snake out, and lap at her hot cunt. He licked languid, deliberate strokes through her folds, savoring the sweet taste of goblin ambrosia: earth and honey. He chirped as liquid bliss coated the inside of his mouth and slid down his throat.

The goblin's moans grew louder. Her toes dug through his feathers as she squirmed against his tongue.

"Aldonas!" she panted, writhing against him. "I'm going to cum on your face!"

Aldonas' cock vibrated faster, growing louder and higher-pitched in time with the goblin's climax. Her back arched and she convulsed wildly, pushing his face firmly against her sex.

She screeched wordlessly until the goblin's trembling ceased. After a few minutes she loosened her grip, falling backward against a large jar of minotaur eyelashes. "Well," she panted, "how do you feel?"

Aldonas shook his head. The hunger subsided, and the

room came back into focus. "M-much better," he stammered. "Thank you. I didn't bite you, did I?"

Dither slid down the ladder, landing silently on the soft wooden floorboards. "Not even a little," she said, pulling on her smallclothes and chemise.

"Oh, good," Aldonas said, locating his own britches. "I was sure I'd bitten you at least a little."

"You bit my dress, my cap, and my hair." Dither spread her arms and spun in a circle for him to observe. "See? No puncture wounds!"

Desire sharpened Aldonas' beak again. The sweet blood rushing through her slender green neck called to him, but he held the hunger at bay. "The accomplishment of a lifetime," he said, rolling his eyes.

"Frog fry!" Dither suddenly squeaked, looking at a large hourglass standing in the corner. "I'm late!" She pulled on her dress and grabbed her caul, rushing back through the maze of magical inventory to the storeroom's entrance. The moment she started moving, Aldonas felt compelled to follow.

The little goblin grabbed small items from shelves, tucking them away inside of her overlarge bell sleeves or shoving them into a canvas bag. Adonas struggled, desperate to keep pace with her as he hopped on one foot, trying to secure his britches.

"Late for what?" he asked, pulling his tunic on. Dither's erratic scurrying made it impossible for him to look away.

"The feast planning meeting!" She threw open the door and raced up the stairs, hastily buttoning up her bodice.

Aldonas lunged after her, nearly pouncing as Dither's tiny frame threatened to disappear into the dark stairwell. "Please don't run," he begged. Aldonas was determined not to lose another battle to his primal hunger.

"I'm sorry?" Dither's pace slowed. "I *am* actually pretty late, though, so maybe just close your eyes, and let me get out of the stairwell?"

Aldonas obeyed, but he could still hear the sounds of clanking metal in her bag growing fainter as the distance between them grew. Fear gripped him, and Aldonas launched himself into the air, flying past her to the first-story landing. From here, he had the high ground and could easily strike.

"It didn't work," he panted, shaking his head, willing the hunger to retreat.

"Alright," Dither said, stepping past him and opening the first-story door. "Maybe I'll just *walk* to the meeting and get there when I get there."

"Thank you," Aldonas said.

They were out in the open now, standing in the bright lights of the great hall of the Academy for the Ethical Advancement of Magic Use. High, vaulted ceilings and magnificent arched windows surrounded them, and as the sun set, enchanted fires sprang to life in the many ornate sconces and hanging lanterns that lined the gleaming sandstone walls. The bright lights helped diffuse Aldonas' focus and temper his need.

Professors, students, and research fellows bustled about, finalizing weekend plans, hurrying to evening study sessions, or simply heading home for the night. But even with everyone present, creatures big and small from all corners of the Three Realms, Aldonas couldn't take his eyes off Dither.

He was transfixed by the way the neckline of her too-large dress slid a little further down her shoulder with every step. He thrilled at the thrum in her throat as her blood lub-dub, lub-dub, lub-dubbed through her veins. He yearned to plunge his copper rod into her slick entrance, coating it in the sweet, earthy smell still lingering on his beak.

"So, like I said," Dither said, readjusting her canvas satchel on her shoulder as she walked slowly to the grand double doors, "I'm going to go to my meeting now, and you're going back upstairs, and you won't have to worry about seeing me again."

"Of course, I've got some papers to grade anyway." Aldonas knew he should turn around, or at the very least, stand still and let the little goblin walk out of his life — but his hunger compelled him forward. When they reached the great oak doors, Aldonas pushed them open, holding one as Dither brushed past onto the rainy front steps, flooding his senses again with almond and earth and honey.

"Thank you again for, um, helping me out ... with my supplies, that is," he said.

"Don't mention it!" Dither replied, stepping out from under the awning and into the rain before a terrible realization struck Aldonas.

"You don't have a cloak!"

"That's all right." Dither trudged on through the rain. "It's not a very long walk. Besides, goblins like to feel a little weather on their face."

Aldonas rushed out to her side. "I'll walk you — just to the meeting house." He stretched a massive wing above her, shielding her from the storm.

Dither smiled and shook her head. "Alright, Mr. *Chivalry*, if you insist."

The pair walked in relative silence through the early evening rain. The island's animals were all tucked away for the winter, and the food vendors and their carts were nowhere to be seen.

Aldonas looked out at the Equiloam Sea: gloomy and dark and still, not a pleasure ship in sight. He'd never much cared for the rainy season — wet feathers, cold talons, short, miserable days — but when he looked over at Dither, dry and safe under his wing, a pride filled his breast, warmer than any summer's day.

Too soon, they reached the council house. Dither climbed the front steps and turned to face him.

"Thank you for walking with me, Aldonas," she said with a

little shrug, "and for letting me cum all over your beak." That cum had permeated his feathers; Aldonas smelled it every time he breathed in.

"I'm sure the pleasure was all mine." His heart lurched when he saw Dither's hand on the doorknob. "And . . . uh, thank *you* for not running."

Dither nodded, "Goodbye forever, then." She smiled and slid silently into the meeting already in progress. That should have been the end of it; Aldonas *should* have gotten on with his evening.

CHAPTER 5

DITHER

The festival planning committee was already there, seated around a large, round table in the center of the leaky stone hut that had been repurposed, after The Peace, as one of the island's many committee spaces. Dither first spotted Drixelorgen the dragonborn: she'd lived on Th'myskôra since before The War; some said she'd lived there even before the trolls first built their sprawling stone city.

Next to her sat Bowen, the pot-bellied, middle-aged satyr who ran the Red Fleet, overseeing imports and exports to and from the island. Then was Arlynn, the pale human woman with fiery red hair, representing the interests of Th'myskôra's local Hedonist Society.

Grenca Wobblepocket — a stout, blonde gnome and the foremost jeweler across the Realms — was always in attendance, representing the interests of the island's many artisans.

Next to her sat Pytr, an awkward young human male who'd recently been appointed head of the park-keepers brigade. And finally, Parvi Florum, the absolutely minuscule flower pixie tasked with coordinating the beautification of the island for every festival.

These were good people, the ones Dither most enjoyed spending time with. They were creative, joyful, and committed to pleasure, just like her.

"Well, hurry up and sit down, Miss Weaselsnout," bellowed Hardwin the manticore as Dither slid into her seat. How could she forget their fearless leader? Hardwin's segmented scorpion tail curled up into attack position reflexively whenever he was annoyed. When Dither was around, it was almost always curled.

"Sorry," she squeaked, setting her damp bag of treasures down on the table.

"Don't listen to him," said Arlynn the human, winking at Dither. "Nobody's said anything important yet anyway."

A giggle filtered through the room before Hardwin rapped his paw on the table. "Order! This assembly *will* come to order! This is our last meeting before the Valentine's Day Feast, and all plans *must* be finalized."

"Very good," said Drixelorgen, taking the floor. "Assss you know, ssspit-roasssting goat on a large ssscale is bessst done out of doors. However, as the winter rainsss are essspecially heavy this year, outdoor roasssting wasss thought imposssssible."

All members of the committee nodded and shuffled respectfully through their notes. Dither nodded along, trying her very best to listen, but water was dribbling in through the cracks in the crude, domed roof and down the uneven walls — it was nearly impossible to pay attention.

"I am pleasssed to report," Drixelorgen continued, "that a partnership between the Ssspiced Goat and Rakka the architect hasss been brokered. He and his aprentisss will be erecting fourteen temporary roasssting shelters along Filfola Road. We will have more than enough food for thisss year's feassst."

"Excellent work," Hardwin said, scribbling something in his notes as those assembled murmured in agreement.

"What about Jack Valentine?" squeaked Dither. "He must have satisfaction!"

Hardwin heaved a sigh. "There are many coexisting cultural and religious traditions represented on the island of Th'myskôra," he said with a flat, practiced affect. "The council recognizes and respects each of those traditions, which is why *you* have been invited to participate in this planning committee, Miss Weaselsnout."

"Great!" Dither hopped up on her chair and dumped her tarnished keys and locks onto the table in a clanging heap. "Now, as you all know, Jack Valentine is a trickster, so in order to properly—"

"*Miss* Weaselsnout!" the imposing manticore interrupted. "We have a very tight schedule this evening. If you will please observe the agenda, you will see that 'satisfying Jack Valentine' is not listed."

"But . . . " Dither's lip quivered as she sat back down.

"I move to *add* it to the agenda!" called Arlynn. "We Hedonists have a vested interest in satisfaction, after all."

"Please," Hardwin grumbled, "can we get through *one* agenda?"

"I second," bellowed Parvi Florum into her minuscule megaphone.

"Do you even know what she wants to do?" Hardwin asked.

Parvi fluttered her gossamer wings, propelling into the air until she was eye to eye with the glowering manticore. Her youthful, cherubic face flashed with indignation. "Don't you talk down to *me*, young man," she shouted. "Things would be running a good sight better on this island if more young people observed the ancient ways."

"Fine." Hardwin ran a massive paw down his face. "If we have time at the end of the meeting, we can talk about Jack Valentine."

"You always say that," Dither protested, "and there's never time!"

The room erupted once more into spirited conversation. Everyone had an opinion on the old ways and the new, on sensuality and free will, on whether the street lamps should come on during midday rainstorms even if it wasn't technically dark out, and on every possible topic of discussion that was *not* listed on the agenda.

"Enough!" Hardwin roared. "I will put Jack Valentine on the official agenda." He pulled out a quill and scribbled hastily at the bottom of the large parchment pinned to the wall behind him. "Now, let's get back on task. Please."

Parvi Florum landed gracefully back on the table, the delicate red petals of her poppy dress fluttering around her.

"The flower pixies have begun beautifying the island. As per the committee's request, we are summoning pink and red flowers. To compensate for this winter's heavy rains, we're focusing on larger, heartier varieties that can stand up to rough weather. You should be seeing them blooming around the island soon."

"Thank you," Hardwin sighed. "Now, Arlynn, your update?"

"Slip-and-fall injuries are likely to be way up this year because of the rain," she said. "Orgies are always slippery, but this one could get out of hand. The Hedonist Society would like four 'No running in the pleasure pit' signs and an extra on-site healer."

"Easy enough," said Hardwin, making a note. "And the pleasure pit will be located . . .?"

"At the southernmost corner of the fairgrounds, behind a fence, with our finest half-orc guarding the entrance. No one wants a repeat of last year." The human shuddered and resumed her seat.

"I should say not," Hardwin grumbled.

Lightning flashed outside, and Dither saw a large, menacing figure lurking beyond the window.

"The storm has turned!" said Grenca, catching water dripping through the thatched roof in the palm of her chubby hand. "We're going to have three hells of a time getting home in this mess."

"Thankfully," said Hardwin, gathering up his things, "we're done. Everyone knows what their responsibilities are moving forward. Everything is in place to ensure that the feast goes off without a hitch."

Thunder cracked. The sound of rain was heavy on the cobblestone path outside the meeting house.

"What about *my* contribution?" squeaked Dither. "We still haven't discussed Jack Valentine!"

The other members of the committee, even outspoken Parvi Florum, were already wrapping themselves in woolen shawls and capes and heading for the door.

There's nothing like a little bad weather to show you who your real allies are.

"Can you make your cassse quickly?" asked Drixelorgen. "These old bones need the comfort of my hearth and a warm fire."

"Yes!" Dither hopped up onto her chair again and snatched

a key and lock, ready to plead her case as quickly as she could. "As you probably know, Jack Valentine is a trickster, especially concerned with the 'accidental pairing' of mortals! For centuries, goblins have honored him on this special day by creeping into houses — preferably through the back door — and leaving wonderful treasures like these!"

She forced a gritty old lock into Grenca's hand and grinned at her, but the plump gnome just blinked.

"Don't you see?" asked Dither impatiently. "This lock corresponds to one of *these* copper keys!" She scurried across the table and smacked a heavy key into Arlynn's hand. "The keys become *keys to the heart* by the will of Jack Valentine!"

She grabbed Arlynn's wrist and Grenca's hand, tugging the two women together.

"Once the artifacts are united," she grunted, forcing the key into the lock, "their owners will be compelled to make mad, passionate love — after which they will be bonded for life!"

Grenca quirked an eyebrow. "Arlynn isn't exactly my type."

"Don't worry," said Dither breathlessly. "It only works during the Valentine's Feast."

"I like the mad lovemaking," said Arlynn thoughtfully. "But how would the participants be decided? Everyone would have to be fully consenting if you want Hedonist approval."

"A lottery?" suggested Bowen.

"Perhaps a matchmaking service," said Grenca, tapping her lip.

"Yes! Yes!" Dither bounced up and down on her toes. "Creatures can enter their names, and Jack Valentine will make the matches!"

"Did you all miss the bit about her using cursed items?" roared Hardwin. "That's poisoning. She wants to poison people!"

"Oh, don't be such a rapture wrecker." Arlynn rolled her eyes. "It's not poisoning if people agree ahead of time."

Another bolt of white lightning flashed outside, and an eerie screech rang through the night.

"Time," croaked Drixelorgen, "isss one thing we do not have. The feassst is in a few short daysss."

"That doesn't matter," said Dither hopefully. "I already have all the supplies, and I'm willing to work day and night to —"

"No," said Hardwin, looking down his muzzle at her. "The potential consequences are too great. *If* we are going to engage in any magical matchmaking, it must be done under the stringent supervision of a *serious* committee."

"But — but . . ." Dither's lip quivered. "Jack Valentine *must* be satisfied."

"Write up a proposal, and we'll see about implementing this . . . *service* next year. Agreed?"

"Agreed!" Echoed the rest of the committee as they shuffled out into the rain, leaving Dither alone in the leaky meeting house.

CHAPTER 6

DITHER

"Wait until next year?" she sniffled. "No one tells the cyclopes they can't slaughter a goat in the eastern caves; no one says the humans can't bury their dead . . . but when it comes to Jack Valentine, *I* have to '*wait for next year*.'"

Dither pressed both hands against the heavy oak door and heaved. "Stupid, giant door," she huffed. "Why isn't anything on this island goblin-sized?" After several harrowing seconds of wielding her entire body weight, the hinges creaked open a few inches, just wide enough for her to squeeze out.

"*Nothing* on this island was built for goblins," she grumbled as she descended the too-tall stone steps.

"Help?" A hulking figure lunged out of the shadows.

"Flippin' frogs!" She screamed and fell backward into a puddle. Dither lifted her sack, ready to swing.

"Sorry, Dither. I hope I didn't frighten you." It was Aldonas, dripping wet, lumbering toward her in the night. "Do you need help?"

"What in three hells are you doing out here in the dark?" Dither said, getting to her feet.

"I'm not sure." Aldonas spread his wing above her head, shielding her from the rain. "I . . . I thought maybe I could walk you home after your meeting. I don't like the idea of you alone out here in this storm."

"Bog forbid." Dither wrung a long stream of muddy water out of her skirts.

Aldonas shifted nervously from one taloned foot to the other, his large, avian head bobbing up and down. "How did your meeting go?"

"Not great," grumbled Dither, stomping in the direction of the forest. Her skirts dragged along the ground, and cold water soaked up the heavy fabric. "You know, back in the old days, when it rained, goblins would just run around naked. But public nudity is frowned upon here on Th'myskôra."

Aldonas cleared his throat before scrambling to catch up with her. "I'm sorry they didn't like your idea."

"Were you listening to the entire meeting?"

"I heard some, through the window," Aldonas admitted. "If it helps, I think the committee is being unfair."

"It's all that Hardwin." Dither kicked a clump of mud. "He's been putting me off for months." The pair turned off the cobblestone street and onto a narrow footpath winding through the glistening, shivering scrub brush.

"First, he said I had to come up with something more *substantial* than 'Jack Valentine must be satisfied,' so I spent weeks combing through the sacred texts, looking for the ritual that would be the best fit for Th'myskôra. Then, when I present the keys and locks, what does he say?"

"No." Aldonas shook his head thoughtfully.

"No! He says, 'We don't have the time,' but that's just an excuse. If I had approval . . . " The path ended at a steep drop-off, and Dither marched down it, her nimble feet finding purchase between roots and rocks with ease.

"Why don't you do it without them?" Aldonas tramped awkwardly downhill after her, struggling to keep his wing extended even as he stumbled and sank into the mud.

"Look at me!" Dither shouted, tears burning her eyes. "I'm just one little goblin. I was a fool to think that *I* could be a worthy acolyte for Jack Valentine."

"I could help you!" Aldonas blurted the words out so quickly, Dither wasn't sure she'd heard him correctly.

"And why would you do that?" Dither eyed him suspiciously.

"I—I just want to help . . ." Aldonas stammered.

"Come to think of it," Dither rounded on him, narrowing her eyes, "what are you doing walking me home? And why were you outside the meeting house? Earlier today, you said you never wanted to see me again, and now you're following me around!"

"I'm—I'm sorry . . ."

"I don't need you to be sorry!" Dither stamped her little foot, smattering both herself and Aldonas with mud. "I need you to tell me what you really want!" She kicked a tree. Hard.

"I . . ." Aldonas clacked his beak nervously. "I — I just want to help you."

"Oh, Bog! I'm sorry!" Dither said as she dropped to her knees in the mud.

"Don't be," Aldonas said sheepishly. "I know I've been giving you mixed signals, and that's not fair."

"Not you — the *tree*!" Dither was caressing it and muttering her apology in ancient Goblish.

"Do you have to use all thirty-eight keys?" Aldonas asked, positioning his wing over her head once again. "Is that the only way to . . . um . . . satisfy Jack Valentine?"

"No." She pulled a snail off a nearby bush and popped it in her mouth, chewing it as she thought aloud. "I suppose just one true love match would do the trick . . . but whoever we find would have to be willing, the committee was *very* clear about that."

Above her, Aldonas' wings fluttered; he chirped and bobbed his head. "What about me? You could find *my* true love match!"

Dither's heart sank.

"Is that what you really want?" She gazed up at him with burning eyes, searching his avian face for some sign of the emotions she hoped he had for her.

"Yes!" Aldonas brayed, offering his wing.

Dither took a deep breath. The thought of pairing Aldonas up with some other woman should have been devastating — but she was *tired*. Tired from a long day at work. Tired of trying to please the festival planning committee. And most of all, she was tired of trying to figure Aldonas out. She didn't have the energy to want him anymore. All Dither could think about in that moment was her den, with its warm, dry nest. Maybe she'd break her own heart the moment she handed him over to some other woman, but at least Jack Valentine would be satisfied.

Dither wrapped her thin green fingers around two of Aldonas' feathers and shook them. "You've got yourself a deal, partner. I'll see you tomorrow morning at the Saffron Smile."

Dither stepped back; she wasn't far from home now. All she had to do was make it back across the invisible line that separated the enchanted Eldrich Forest from the rest of the island, and she'd be free. She could be as sad as she wanted in the safety of her own den, but Aldonas wasn't letting her go. Every time she stepped away, he advanced.

Dither took another clumsy step backward. Her foot slipped on a slick rock, and she slid down the hill behind her, scraping her knees against rocks and smashing her elbows on roots as she tumbled faster and faster. The world was a blur of mud, trees, and night. Her caul snagged on a branch. Dither clawed at the earth, desperate to slow her descent, but she was powerless to save herself.

"SCREEE!"

Before Dither could understand what was happening, razor-sharp talons ripped through her wet woolen dress — she'd been plucked from her brutal descent. Aldonas released her with a thud onto a dense carpet of wild mint and stood possessively over her body. She quivered when his huge, clawed foot pinned her to the ground, his deadly beak hovering only inches from her throat. She wanted him to strike. She needed him to want her.

Dither was on flat ground now, only a few feet from the tree line. If she could wriggle free, she was sure she'd make it across the barrier — but she just didn't want to.

Aldonas reared back, his beak glistening in the rain. He lunged forward, plunging into — not her supple green flesh, but her sopping wet overdress. Aldonas' beak ripped through the fabric as his head raced down the length of her bodice. He sliced open not only her dress, but also her chemise and small-clothes, exposing her tender flesh to the chill of the pounding, biting rain.

"Aldonas, wait," Dither said as calmly as she could, fighting her own raging, carnal need.

His eyes flashed up to her face, and she was transfixed. Dither's mouth watered, and her sex began to swell, calling out for him, demanding service.

As abruptly as he'd attacked, Aldonas stumbled backward off of her, shaking his head. "Dither, you're naked! I'm so sorry. Did I hurt you?"

"Come here!" she demanded, and Aldonas obeyed. She got to her feet and yanked both his britches and smallclothes down, revealing his shining, copper cock. It was already vibrating, singing just for her. "Sit down," she instructed, and again Aldonas obeyed, lowering himself onto the fragrant green earth.

"Tomorrow, we can find you a love match," Dither said. "But tonight, you're mine." She stood astride his hips, placing her hands on his shoulders.

"Tonight, I'm yours," Aldonas repeated, lying back into the mint.

Dither lowered herself onto him, struggling to straddle his broad hips. The closer she got to his cock, the louder it sang. The louder it sang, the more she ached for him.

Dither crushed mint leaves under her toes, sending plumes of fragrance into the frigid night air. Rainwater soaked her hair and streamed down her face, leaving the soft kiss of almond oil on her lips. Warm, pillowy feathers brushed against her inner thighs as she wriggled and maneuvered into position. He was so large that her knees didn't reach the ground, and she had to squeeze her thighs around him for stability.

Aldonas' hard, metal cock lurched upward, smacking her on the ass. It was even colder than the rain pummeling her tender flesh.

Dither placed her hands on the impossibly broad expanse of his torso. She balled her fists, gripping his damp cotton tunic and arched her back, angling her ass, sliding it against the smooth, metallic member.

Aldonas cooed, and his feathers bristled beneath her. Dither shuddered at his touch. He was soft and warm, and she was safe, feeling his downy feathers all over her body. She'd been dreaming of what it might be like to be wrapped up in his wings since she first saw him, and it was easy to imagine it lasting forever.

Stop daydreaming, Dither. This is the last time.

Aldonas wrapped his massive wings around her, encasing her in a downy dome of pleasure. The sound of the rain was muffled, drowned out by Aldonas' ringing cock and her own moans. She shifted against his dick, sliding her sex along its turgid length, coating it with her desire.

"Dither," Aldonas croaked, bucking his pelvis under her, smacking his cock against her swollen, wet clit. "I want *you!*"

"Don't rush me," she admonished, shoving a finger in his

face. "You've been playing with me for years; tonight, I'm going to get what *I* want."

Aldonas groaned, but lay still under her, and Dither readjusted herself. She leaned to the side, placing one foot fully on the ground, and put her other knee on top of his massive thigh. "Now I can get to work!"

Dither reached beneath her, grabbing Aldonas' cock firmly in her grip.

The singing changed pitch.

She pressed her opening to the bulbous copper head, and the frequency changed again. Dither yipped as she pressed the vibrating tip against her opening. The musical buzzing of his cock radiated through her cunt, making her clit vibrate even though it wasn't touching it.

Aldonas groaned, and Dither rocked her hips, working the shining, vibrating penis further inside her canal. Once she'd gotten it properly situated, the sensation changed: Aldonas' cock was vibrating not only her sex, but also her thighs. She worked it in a little further, grinding the shimmering rod against her G-spot.

"How . . . how are you doing that?" She panted as the vibrations spread through her pelvis, pleasure filling her belly and flickering through her asshole.

Aldonas didn't answer. His eyes were wild. He nipped at the loose strands of Dither's hair that dragged across his face as he bucked underneath her, plunging his singing cock deeper and deeper into her tiny body.

Dither's breath caught in her throat. She worried he might tear her apart, but the pleasure was worth the risk. She balled her fists, grabbing onto his tunic with all her might. Her muscles seized, and her back arched. The cold, hard rod lurched inside of her, banging and thrashing. The new sensation sent her over the edge. Dither climaxed as Aldonas shot torrents of glittering cum, filling her pussy. The musical vibrations spread through her entire body. When Dither opened her mouth to gasp out her orgasm, a flurry of beautiful, colored light spilled out into the feathered cocoon of their shared ecstasy.

Aldonas' cock stilled inside of her. Slowly, Dither stood, wobbly-kneed on the thighs of the giant, spent strix. His feathers now returned to their customary brown, his black pupils once again tracking her every move.

"Well, that was . . . " *Amazing? Soul-destroying? The best orgasm of my life?*

"It was a mistake, Dither," Aldonas said, lifting her gently by the waist and placing her on the ground. "One I can't make again."

"Yes!" Dither squeaked, gathering up her things, covering herself with her ruined dress. "A huge, stupid mistake." She turned away and started walking toward the forest.

"Dither wait," Aldonas tried to follow, but tripped on the britches still bunched around his ankles. "That's not what I meant!"

"Tomorrow we can find your love match, and you can forget this ever happened — I know I will!"

Before she had to suffer one more squawk, Dither rushed past the tree line, back to the safety of the woods.

CHAPTER 7

ALDONAS

"Rh'ibble, droke-droke, wraalg," said the blue grung as he set a large pot of tea and two earthenware cups on the little white table in the corner of the vine-encircled courtyard.

"Drālg! Rhaggul bk'bk! Proargerg druke." Dither replied, and the grung inclined his squat head before hopping back across the courtyard and into the Saffron Smile.

Aldonas stared across the table, his beak agape.

"I hope you don't mind me ordering for us," said Dither, blushing.

"N-no! Thank you." Aldonas poured each of them a cup of mint tea. "I've never heard grung spoken before. When I come here, the waiter just nods at me." The thought of Dither sharing a secret language with another male sent the tiniest pang of jealousy loose in his mind.

"Yeah," Dither said, stirring some sugar into her tea. "Ever since the elvish occupation of Grung'lund, they're very suspicious of outsiders. But we children of the forest always find a way to communicate."

"Fascinating." Aldonas took his first sip of piping-hot tea; the smell and taste of mint transported him immediately back to the ecstasy he'd found between Dither's thighs.

I didn't eat her. I didn't even bite her last night. I shouldn't tempt fate. I should leave now, while I still can.

But Aldonas didn't leave. He breathed in his tea deeply and stared at her face, imagining it twisted in agonizing pleasure as he drove his cock relentlessly inside of her.

"Nice of the rain to give us a break today." Aldonas set his cup down. The sky was a brilliant, piercing blue, the kind you only get to see between storms.

"I'll say!" Dither stirred some more sugar into her tea. "If it were still raining, we'd have to sit inside, and this patio is in the absolute perfect location for spying on people!" Dither giggled, and the sound sent desire coursing through Aldonas' veins.

Whatever you say, it can't be, "I want to rip out your entrails and wear them like a hat."

"I thought you brought us here for him," Aldonas whispered conspiratorially, quirking his head in the direction of the kitchen.

"d'Iehb?" Dither laughed. "He's got two husbands *and* a wife at home!"

"Whoa! Save a couple mates for the rest of us, am I right?" Relief washed over Aldonas when Dither's disinterest in the little frogman became apparent.

Mine.

She laughed again, and her tiny chest shook, her bulbous eyes gleamed, and she snorted, just a little, at the end.

Aldonas' cock stirred.

"Proargerg, wraalg." d'Iehb the grung was back with two deep dishes: braised baby rabbits for Aldonas, and custard with boiled fruit fashioned into a face and drenched in honey for Dither. "Drālg."

"Drālg!" said Dither, grabbing her spoon and digging in.

"Dragle?" asked Aldonas. "Does that mean thank you?"

"Drālg," Dither corrected around a mouthful of candied pear. "The closest translation into common tongue would be something like: *appreciation should be present.* But it's probably better to think of it as please, thank you, and you're welcome."

"Fascinating." Aldonas lowered his head, opened his beak, and slid a baby rabbit down his throat. "The best braised rabbit in the Realms is right here on Th'myskôra."

If the gods have any pity for me at all, this flesh will temper my hunger.

"What about *her*?" Dither practically leaped out of her chair, and Aldonas' head slid back and forth on his neck as his large, yellow eyes tracked her every move.

A handsome female ogre of a certain age was strolling past the patio. She was tall, sturdily built, and dressed in a fine white satin gown, the hem of which dragged through the remnants of last night's puddles. But Aldonas was transfixed by Dither— he could snap her delicate neck with one bite from his powerful jaws.

"Tender, raw, supple . . ." Aldonas muttered.

Dither stared blankly at him.

"That is . . . " Aldonas shook his head and blinked, willing the hunger away. "Ogres only wear white during the third year of mourning. *She* won't be ready to even *think* about romance again for another decade."

"What about *you*?" Dither asked brightly.

"Me? I'm not in mourning! Why would I be? No one's died. I — I haven't eaten a single person!"

"What?" Dither slid another spoonful of custard past her lips. "Oh, sorry. I went back to languages. Do you speak any besides the common tongue? What does strix language sound like?"

"Oh, um . . . it's mostly screeching. Shades of meaning are conveyed by volume."

"Say something!"

"I'm . . . uh . . . I'm not fluent." Guilt bubbled up inside him, temporarily overshadowing his hunger. "My parents never spoke it at home."

"Oh," Dither said, patting him on the back of the wing. "I'm sorry."

Her touch was intoxicating. Aldonas' culmen threatened to elongate, and his gape watered.

Not as sorry as you're going to be if you keep touching me.

Aldonas pulled his wing back and folded it across his lap. "I do remember a few words my grandmother taught me."

I could have learned more. I should have spent more time with her; she was right there, right down the road.

"Like what?" Dither's large eyes blinked up at him expectantly. He wanted to pluck those eyes right out of her pretty little head and eat them. He wanted to make love to her. He wanted to protect her.

What is happening to me? Why does Dither inspire such powerful and conflicting feelings?

"Schriiiihck!" Aldonas called from a forgotten place deep in his throat — it was a word he hadn't uttered once in all the years since his grandmother died.

"Like this?" Dither took a deep breath and braced her hands on the table. "Schriiiick!"

"Louder. Schriiiick!"

"Schriiiick!" the little goblin bellowed, her face upturned, her eyes squeezed shut.

"Perfect," Aldonas said, beaming at his eager pupil, his copper cock thrumming.

"Schriiiick! Schriiiick!" Dither practiced her new word with perfect diction, and Aldonas treasured the sound ringing in his ears,

"Schriiiick!" he called back to her, their voices echoing through the streets.

"What does it mean?" Dither finally asked.

"I love you." Aldonas felt his face heat under his feathers.

Dither blushed too, and then her eyes dropped to her breakfast as she shoveled another heaping spoonful of custard into her mouth.

"We should probably leave," she said, licking her spoon clean. "I don't think your love match is likely to just plop down to eat in this courtyard." She stood to leave, but Aldonas' sharp eyes didn't miss her slipping the pewter spoon into her over-sized bell sleeve.

"Wait!" Aldonas called, tipping his head back and swallowing the last of his rabbits. "You can't take that."

"But it's so shiny," Dither whined, gazing up at him.

Aldonas heaved a sigh. "If you want new spoons, visit the cutler; you're only making more work for the grungs this way."

"All right, *Mr. Rules.*" Dither shook her arm over the table, letting the spoon, two knives, and the sugar bowl clatter out onto the table. "The sooner I get you partnered up and out of my mycelium, the better!"

The two of them walked down Filfola Street, past an eclectic assemblage of earthen, stone, and stick-built structures, through the growing Saturday morning crowd. Each time they passed a female of any species, Dither stopped, clasped her tiny hands over her chest, and muttered something. After each one, she sighed, shook her head, and kicked at the mud.

There was a shapely basilisk sweeping the front steps of Mimple's Toy Shoppe.

"No good."

And a lithe cockatrice stumbling nervously out of Grond's Wands, the island's *adult* toy store.

"Not her either."

Finally, after Dither turned her nose up at an elegant, pink tiefling walking a pharaoh hound on a long leather lead, Aldonas asked, "What is it that you're looking for exactly?"

"I'm not looking," Dither said. "I'm asking Jack Valentine if I've found your match! He is a trickster, after all, and a trickster loves a guessing game."

They turned onto Zeluk Row and walked toward the fairgrounds, the future site of the pleasure pit where Aldonas was expected to bind himself for all of time to a complete stranger in just a few days.

What in all the realms possessed me to volunteer for that?

"Uh . . . Dither?" Aldonas asked, stopping between her and the Peerless Bauble — Grenca Wobblepocket's jewelry shop. "What if I don't have a match?"

"You shut your filthy frogging mouth, Aldonas Strigidae!" Dither stamped her little foot and spoke very quickly. "Everyone has a true love match; in fact, everyone has two or three *dozen* potential true love matches. It's only a matter of meeting one of them at the *right* time, under the *right* conditions."

"Yes," Aldonas said, even though he didn't believe in Jack Valentine, Dither's dedication was endearing. "But what if none of *my* matches are here on Th'myskôra?" As much as he wanted to make her happy, Aldonas hoped she wouldn't be able to find him a match.

Dither closed her eyes and clasped her hands over her chest. "Jack Valentine, you mighty sprite, I wish to satisfy your will. Does this strix have a true love match living here on the island of Th'myskôra right now?"

She hummed a little song and swayed back and forth for what seemed like an extremely long time. Aldonas' eyes were fixed on her, registering every subtle movement, every shift of her body weight. He found himself planning for her next move at every moment.

She must not escape.

Aldonas had to watch the crowd, too — parcel-laden creatures and craftsmen bustling past, many of them large: griffins, minotaurs, trolls. There were potential predators everywhere.

She will not be taken.

Dither's eyes flew open. "You definitely have a true love match here!" she squealed. "I can feel her presence strongly — she is likely standing on this very street!"

Aldonas swallowed hard. "Dither, what if I'm not ready to bond to a mate?"

"You're not thinking of squirming out of helping me, are you?" She waggled her slender finger in his face, practically begging him to bite it off.

"Not at all," he lied.

"Good, because Jack Valentine *must* be satisfied!" A righteous blush made her cheeks burn every time she spoke of her sacred duty. Aldonas was beginning very much to look forward to seeing that blush.

"It's just . . . " Aldonas sighed. "There are things you don't know about me — dark, dangerous things."

Dither scrambled up the little staircase in front of the Peerless Bauble. Aldonas' eyes darted back and forth, noting every move.

She took his wing in her hands and stroked it. "Being someone's true love match doesn't mean being perfect, or even a perfect version of yourself. It just means that the two of you are perfect *for each other*."

They were face-to-face now. All he would have to do was open his beak. He could snap her up in an instant. "Dither, you don't understand —"

"Don't worry," she said, raising a hand to silence him. "When you meet your true love match, all of this hesitation will melt away. You'll be drawn to each other, and you'll want to spend the rest of your life together. By the time you're standing in the pleasure pit on Valentine's Day, you'll be begging to bond with your love match."

As she spoke, her touch lingered, fingers carefully caressing his feathers. Aldonas was flooded with hunger, with need for her.

"Get away from me," he suddenly pleaded, voice creaking. Iron-grey clouds crowded the sky overhead.

"Aldonas," Dither said, gently releasing his wing and taking a step back. "You're making that face again."

CHAPTER 8

DITHER

Dither's heart pounded, and her sex thrummed as she ran down Zeluk Road, zipping past stone huts, earthen structures, and stick-built shops. Every storefront she passed got her closer to making another wonderful, carnal mistake with Aldonas.

Her soft moss-lined feet bounced off the cobbles as thunder rumbled and the wind picked up, ruffling her hair and threatening to blow away her caul as she ran. There were only four shops between her and the muddy fairground.

She knew he'd chase her.

She knew he'd catch her.

Dither darted between a family of fawns leaving Luther's Flutes. Aldonas lumbered behind her on feet made for striking, not locomotion.

She splashed through an icy puddle, spraying mud across the red front door of the Winking Shrew.

"We're never going to find your match if you keep chasing me like this!" she shouted over her shoulder, nearly knocking into Holly, the buxom cyclops who managed The Iron Axe Head.

"Watch yourself!" Holly barked, cracking her knuckles as Dither barreled past.

"Screeee!" Aldonas' primal screech echoed in her large, pointed ears.

The park-keepers' Valentine's preparations were well underway, but they didn't work on Saturdays. The pitch would be empty.

Dither darted behind a large pile of lumber under a canvas tarp just in time to see Aldonas soar overhead: mighty wings outstretched, eyes wild, and copper cock practically bursting through his britches.

He circled the fairgrounds — once, twice, three times — before settling in a tree on the edge of the muddy field.

"Dither!" he screeched. "I told you not to run from me!" His large, flat face twisted, and his massive, round head swiveled on his neck, piercing eyes searching for her among the not-yet-assembled tents and wooden crates stuffed with banners and flags.

She savored the primal sound of her name ripping through

the gloomy afternoon sky. "If you don't want me to run," Dither goaded, "then stop looking at me like you want to eat me!"

Aldonas' head snapped in the direction of the lumber pile.

"Mine." His voice cut through the clearing as he launched his powerful body toward her.

Dither grinned, her pulse thrumming through her slickening cunt. She gathered up her skirts and ran, full speed. Massive, soundless wings sliced through the air, and lightning flashed through clouds dense with the weight of an impending storm. Dither's toes sank into the mud as she charged toward the future site of the pleasure pit.

"Stop!" Aldonas commanded. He tore through the darkening sky, diving talons-first. Dither kept running, her eyes fixed on the huge, muddy puddle in the southernmost corner of the fairgrounds.

Aldonas narrowly missed her, crashing into a wooden barrel that cracked and splintered under his weight. Its contents went flying, mallets and lengths of rope now littering the ground.

"Pull yourself together!" Dither panted, looking over her shoulder at a blood-red Aldonas shaking mud from his feathers. She was still running when he flapped his mighty wings and disappeared into the murky grey sky above. "We don't have much time left!" Dither grinned.

Just enough time for me to ride that shining, smooth cock one more time.

Dither stopped in a large open expanse of fairground. Muddy water pooled around her ankles, staining the hems of her skirts.

It's time to get caught.

She twirled happily through the soggy yellow grass and muck, letting her heavy skirts spin. She tilted her face and closed her eyes, letting the fine mist of fresh rainwater coat her face.

Any moment now . . .

"Why don't you come down here, Aldonas?" she goaded. "We can talk this over rationally!"

PHUAMP!

Aldonas crashed into her tiny body, knocking her hard to the ground. Dither was surrounded by feathers, encased in his wings. She closed her eyes and felt his soft down caressing her face. Her ass was fully submerged in mud, and the standing water soaked through her heavy woolen dress, her cotton chemise, and even her smallclothes.

"You shouldn't have run," Aldonas growled in her ear.

"What are you going to do now that you've caught me?" Dither's mouth watered as her fingers searched frantically through his clothes for her prize.

"Feast!"

Aldonas reared back, revealing his monstrous face, features warped and exaggerated with need. His pupils had disappeared. His beak had grown long and deadly sharp. Aldonas clicked it open and closed, bobbing his head toward her, threatening to bite.

"You are not allowed to eat me," Dither said firmly, staring into the horrifying magnificence of his empty, yellow eyes.

Aldonas threw his head back. He screeched and flapped his wings wildly, splashing muddy water high into the air.

"Only sex," Dither said, raising an eyebrow and wagging her finger.

The words had barely passed her lips when Aldonas thrust himself upon her. He tore at her bodice with his beak, shredding the wool, stripping layers of fabric from her quivering, green body.

Each time his cold, hard maxilla grazed her skin, Dither's sex fluttered. She'd known the pleasures provided by the copper-dicked owl, and every part of her being ached to know them again.

Dither scrambled to her feet, weighed down by her sopping wet, tattered skirts. "I'm going to undress you now, and you're going to behave," she ordered.

Aldonas chirped impatiently. He scratched at the mud with his deadly talons as Dither untied the waistbands of his britches and smallclothes.

She slowly slid his clothes down. There was Aldonas' gleaming copper cock, freed from its hiding place just for her.

"Boilin' bog," she whispered, wide-eyed. "That's got to be *the* shiniest penis anywhere in the Three Realms." She guided his feet out of his britches and stood again to remove his cloak and tunic. "No sense in both of our clothes getting ruined."

"W-what?" Aldonas shook his head — his pupils were back. "Oh, Dither! Your dress is ruined! Did I do that?"

Dither stood in the rain, struggling to pull the heavy woolen dress over her head. "Just help me get this thing off!"

Aldonas rushed to her aid and tugged it free in one smooth motion. "We probably shouldn't . . . I don't want to hurt you."

The sky split open, and rain rushed fiercely down, pelting their shivering, quivering bodies. Dither wore no chest bindings, and her cotton chemise, now slashed, was growing less opaque by the second. She felt her nipples tighten against the rough, wet cotton and saw Aldonas' hungry gaze linger on them.

"What *do* you want?" Dither stared into Adonas' eyes, daring him to attack. The sky was blackened by storm clouds, but she had no doubt that he could see her perfectly.

"I want . . ."

Dither tore off her tattered chemise. Aldonas' black pupils receded, gleaming yellow conquered his eyes once more. Dither crouched, fumbling through the mud until she found a smooth, flat rock that fit perfectly in her hand.

"I want *you!*" He lunged at her, but Dither was faster. She rushed forward, rock in hand, and knocked it against his cock. A beautiful, clear chime rang out, and Aldonas stopped dead in his tracks. She hit his cock with the rock again, and a higher, sweeter note sounded.

"I found an ancient text about copper-dicked owls," Dither explained, grinning, and she struck his cock again.

"How . . ." Aldonas was dazed. "How are you doing that? My mind, it . . . it's . . . I can *speak*."

"It turns out," said Dither, sliding one careful finger up his wet, vibrating cock, "that a strix can be tamed." She chimed his dick again. "If a skilled partner plays his cock properly, she can redirect his need for flesh into pure sexual power."

"Dither," Aldonas puffed out his feathers and raised his wings, towering over her. "Play it again."

"Master the dix, master the strix!" She struck his shining cock and laughed.

Aldonas tackled her, and she fell backward with a terrific splash. He knelt in the mud, grabbed her from the back of each knee, and pulled her body hard into his.

Dither lay in the icy mud, squinting against the rainwater crashing down on her face, a jagged rock clutched in her tiny fist.

"This is perfect," she squeaked. Aldonas' chest rose and fell with wild, ragged breaths. Dither watched him shudder for her, her sex growing slicker in response.

He stared at her through those terrible, frightening yellow eyes, and her clit throbbed. Her whole body ached for him, as it had for years — since the first time she saw him.

The rain was brutal now, coming down in sheets, but every freezing droplet that pelted her delicate skin brought with it as much delicious pleasure as thrilling pain.

Just one more indiscretion before I hand him over to a proper match at the Valentine's Feast.

Rain bounced off his vibrating cock, and each drop that struck the sonorous metal echoed through the air like a tiny bell. Every chime was part of an erotic enchantment meant just for her.

"Fuck me, Aldonas!"

Aldonas dragged his hard, gleaming cock through her pubic hair. It was dripping wet and freezing cold, and Dither quaked as he slid it along her lips, brushing it ever so briefly against her clit.

"Mine!" he shrieked as he pulled her hips higher into the air. He pressed the hollow tip of his still-vibrating cock to her opening, and Dither gasped.

"It's like ice!"

He plunged it inside her — one desperate, animal thrust, and half of his cock was buried, making her cunt vibrate from the inside. Icy cold coursed through her body, chilling her inner walls and adding the pulsing thrum of her own greedy cunt to the music emanating from him.

The further Aldonas pushed his metal rod inside Dither's body, the more of his vibration she felt.

When he rammed his tip against her cervix, Dither's breath caught. Her entire body trembled and pulsed in harmony with the beautiful sound of his perfect cock.

"Is that all of it?" She panted, struggled, and gulped for breath.

Aldonas nodded. He started moving the thing inside her slowly, carefully. His wings tightened around her thighs, and he grunted with each pump.

"I — I need to," Aldonas stuttered. "Can I go faster?"

"Yes." Dither nodded, lost in the terrible yellow pools of his eyes. Aldonas' pace quickened. She needed him to know that she liked it. That he wasn't being too rough with her. That she didn't want him to stop. "Harder," she whimpered. "You can fuck me harder than that."

Aldonas screeched, bucking wildly up into her. With each powerful stroke, he fucked the song of his copper cock deeper into her core. Each time his soft, feathery pelvis met her dripping sex, Dither's pleasure coiled more tightly inside her.

Her arousal coated his cock, dripping down his red feathers and mixing with the pools of rainwater. She dug her fingers into the sodden earth beneath her. Desperate to give more of herself to him, she opened her mouth to scream, but heard the magical chimes of Aldonas' cock reverberating out through her own throat. She squeezed her eyes shut as her breath caught and her back arched. Her orgasm crashed through her tiny body as Aldonas ruined her in the mud.

Dither had only started to come down from her climax, was still spasming in the mud, when Aldonas slid his metal rod out of her.

"Wait," she cried, "I can go again, you need to —" before her sentence was finished, he'd flipped her over. Dither's hands and cheek were pressed into the mud. Her ass was high in the air.

Aldonas wrapped his silken feathers around either side of her hips and slammed his dripping copper dick back inside of her.

With each thrust, she felt his hard, vibrating balls tap against her clit.

"SCREEEEEECH!"

Aldonas held Dither's ass flush against his crotch as his cock thumped inside of her, releasing thick, viscous cables of glittering cum.

The feeling of her face sliding in the mud, of his cock pounding inside her, the satisfaction that he was filling *her* with his seed — pushed Dither over the peak of climax again. She came on his cock, face down in the mud. Her fluid mixed with his, overflowing out of her cunt and running down the backs of her legs.

Spent, Aldonas rolled onto his back. He pulled Dither into the warmth of his chest and gently wrapped them both up in his wings. The vibrating in his cock had ceased, his breathing was slowing, and his eyes were back to normal.

"Now I owe you two dresses," he cooed in her ear.

"It's okay," said Dither brightly. "I needed shredded strips of wool for a project anyway."

Aldonas laughed. "You like to keep busy, don't you?"

"I like you," said Dither, closing her eyes and snuggling into Aldonas' feathers. "You're soft."

CHAPTER 9
ALDONAS

Aldonas felt the rising sun warm his face as he lay on the soft, wet ground, trampled soggy grass crushed beneath his naked, muddy body. The now familiar scents of warm earth, honey, and almond hair oil floated up from Dither's cozy little body.

Yesterday, the fairgrounds had been streaked with bitter rain, a hunting field through which his prey had scurried in a futile attempt to escape his razor-sharp grasp. This morning, the scrub brush that surrounded the field teemed with life and new possibilities. There were budding peonies and dahlias all around. Everywhere he looked, Aldonas could see bright pink flowers begging to bloom, eager to share their beauty with the world.

As he lay under a soft blanket of misty morning fog, Aldonas looked over the fairgrounds that would soon be teeming with activity. It was easy for him to imagine strolling through the festival with Dither's little hand clasped in his wing. Now that she'd calmed his bloodlust, anything was possible.

Dither stirred. She was curled up in his feathers, warm and cooing against his breastbone.

I never would have thought snoring could be cute. Of course, I never would have thought that I'd wake up naked in a muddy field holding a goblin, either.

A feeling of complete contentment and peace washed over him.

So small. So fragile.

He ran a feather gently down the side of her face. For the first time since Dither had come to work at the Academy, Aldonas wasn't fighting the urge to devour her.

"Fascinating," he murmured into the top of her head, nuzzling his beak against her mossy green locks. "Fascinating and wonderful." She was still clutching her flat, grey rock in her tiny green hands as she slept.

For thirty years, I've struggled to control my hunger, and this resourceful little imp has discovered the cure in only a few days. Maybe she, herself, is the cure . . . perhaps she was all along.

The first time Aldonas had seen Dither scurry through a crowded hallway, she had been impossible to ignore. He'd tried to convince himself that it was only the erratic way she hurried from one dark corner to the next, arousing his instinct to chase small mammals,   but *that* was an urge he was usually able to suppress. No, there was something deeper about his desire for Dither, beyond his primal, animal hunger. Cradling her in his wings, Aldonas had the feeling that he was holding an extension of himself.

"Mmmmm . . . Jack," Dither mumbled in her sleep. "Jack Valentine."

Then, on that fateful day two summers ago, she'd made the mistake of running from him into the live oak grove.

That was the best mistake of my life, maybe of both of our lives . .
.

When Dither had looked up at him with her large, round, wet eyes, her full, pouty lip quivering, her disheveled, too-large dress falling below her shoulder and revealing her delicious décolletage, his desire to feed had been joined by an equally powerful need to mate. A desire to possess her, to fill her with his copper rod and hear her cries of brutal pleasure and divine pain.

Now he'd had her. *Really* had her.

Or has she had me?

Dither rolled over on his chest and ran her free hand through his feathers. "Soft," she murmured. "That's *my* soft."

As long as Dither controls my cock, it can't control me. I can have everything: a respectable career and a loving, stable home. I won't have to lurk in the shadows, forced to hunt and feed under the cover of night. I won't have to live like a strix, like a monster. As long as I have Dither, and she has that rock, we can be normal together.

"All right, boys! Let's get these holes dug and these poles in the ground before it starts raining again!"

Aldonas' eyes snapped open. He tightened his grip around Dither and sprang to his feet.

"Whas . . . what's going on?" she asked, bleary-eyed.

"Park-keepers!" Aldonas tried to keep his voice down to avoid detection, but the terror rising in his throat was undeniable.

"Is it morning? Did we fall asleep in the pleasure pit?" Dither asked, giggling. "I honestly didn't think you had it in you." She patted Aldonas lightly on the chest.

In the distance, through the early morning fog, Aldonas could see a dozen workers — mostly humans, or human-shaped, at least.

"We've got to get out of here!" he shrieked.

"Don't worry," Dither said, swinging her feet through the air. "I checked the bylaws. The fairground is open to the public unless there's an active festival. The Valentine's Feast won't be considered active until the main tent is erected. So . . . likely sometime this afternoon, but there's absolutely no way that we can get in trouble for the sex we had last night, or even for sleeping here!"

"Dither. We are naked and covered in mud. *That* is the trouble." He pointed a wing at the impending work crew, trudging across the field towards them.

"Well, put me down and get dressed if you're so worried about it."

"Wow!" shouted a not-distant-enough voice. "What happened *here* last night?"

"It was raining hard, but not *that* hard!" said a husky female voice. The crew had reached the shattered barrel, the one Aldonas had crashed into during last night's crazed pursuit.

"Britches!" Aldonas dug through the mud wildly, scratching with his talons and pecking the ground with his beak. "I've got to find my britches!"

"It looks like some kind of animal came through here!" said the first park-keeper. "Thomas, would you go check on the giant shrew stables?"

"Sure thing, boss!"

"Gods save me!" Aldonas spotted the hem of his woolen britches, crushed into a mound of half-dried mud. He pulled them up with the tips of his wings and found his white cotton smallclothes tucked inside. "They're soaked through!"

Aldonas chose to forgo his sopping wet underclothes and step directly into his muddy britches.

"They'll be here any minute," he muttered, pulse racing, heartbeat pounding in his ears.

He shivered as he pulled them up and felt hard clumps of

caked-on mud scraping against his bare lower legs. "It's better than nothing," he said, looking desperately for his tunic. "How about you, Dither? There's got to be *something* of that dress left!"

When he looked up at her, the little goblin was standing completely still, staring at his crotch and pouting.

"Your dick went away," she said, sex rock clutched to her chest.

"What?" Aldonas was breathing fast and shallow. His head was beginning to spin.

"Your copper cock," she whined. "It's away in its little bird pouch."

"Don't worry about this lumber now, boys!" Called the first park-keeper. "Let's get over to the pleasure pit; those holes need to be twenty-three inches deep. I don't want to be out here all day."

"Of course it's away," Aldonas snapped. "We're in a real situation here!"

"But . . . but I thought I was the special stimuli—"

"You *were!*" Aldonas turned away from her, frantically clawing through the mud, looking for the tattered remains of her dress.

"But not anymore?"

"Hey, what's this?" asked a familiar male voice.

"Looks like a cloak," someone answered. "A really big cloak."

"We can talk about this later, Dither," Aldonas hissed. "Right now, I need you to help me!"

"Dither? Dither is that you?" It was too late. Pytr, the gangly pink human who'd been barking orders since the work crew arrived, had seen them — worse, he'd recognized Dither.

"Good morning, Pytr," she said, sniffling and wiping her nose with the back of her hand as she walked over to the work crew.

"Wow," the young human said, running his five human fingers through his hair. "You kept saying that you wanted to satisfy Jack Valentine, but I didn't think you meant . . . *personally.*"

The other park-keepers all laughed, and Dither smiled up at Pytr, her dazzling white teeth shining past the mud.

He's looking at her. They're all looking at her.

Aldonas' vision narrowed on Dither as jealousy sharpened his talons.

"This probably seems *pretty silly* . . . " she chuckled, planting her tiny green fists on her soft, slim hips. "But there's a perfectly normal explanation."

A beam of early morning light broke through the fog and danced along Dither's perfect body. Timid sunshine crept down her delicate neck, over her perky green breasts, and tight pink nipple buds. It shone along her sculpted midsection and illuminated the forest of wild green pubic hair that a few short hours ago had been Aldonas' refuge.

"*Mine!*" Aldonas shrieked. He flew between them and thrust his wings around her, pulling his goblin away from the group of interlopers.

"Let go of me!" Dither struggled against his wings, but Aldonas was stronger. "I am *trying* to have a conversation!"

"He was looking at you," Aldonas said. "They're *all* looking at you!"

"Pytr happens to be a friend of mine," Dither grunted, still unable to free herself. "Can you just be normal about this?"

"Can *I* be normal? You're having nude, muddy conversations with workmen, and you're telling *me* to be normal?"

"The lady said hands off." Pytr took a step forward, brandishing a shovel. "We're not going to have a problem, are we?"

Several of the other park-keepers moved in closer. Some were holding mallets, others shovels or lengths of lumber. Aldonas felt his pupils disappear. He would tear each one of these rivals apart if they tried to take her from him.

"Professor Strigidae?" It was Grover Gribble, the were-vole from Aldonas' introduction to blood magic class, standing with the work crew, holding something … something soft. "I think I found your tunic — over there, in the mud."

Aldonas was knocked instantly back to his senses. He was standing shirtless, covered in mud, restraining a naked, squirming goblin in front of one of his students. Shame pulled all the heat from his face and twisted in his gut. Aldonas let his wings fall. Dither stomped a couple of angry feet away, and Pytr and the other park-keepers lowered their weapons.

"I'm sorry," said Grover, handing the ruined garment to Aldonas. "I think it's ripped."

"Thank you, Mr. Gribble."

CHAPTER 10

DITHER

Storm clouds were gathering overhead, as dark and turbulent as the storm raging inside of Dither herself.

"Don't give it a second thought . . . Grover, was it?" Dither strode over to the trembling youth and placed a comforting hand on his arm. "Torn tunics and wild muddy nights are all just part of life." She saw the were-vole's pulse quicken at his temple the moment she touched him. She knew that Aldonas saw it too.

Good. A bitter thought streaked across her mind. *It's about time Aldonas sees what it feels like when he can't control the situation.*

"Dither," Aldonas said, his voice barely audible through his clenched beak. "Will you please come over here and cover up?"

She didn't turn to address him. "You seemed to think public nudity was fine when you were *hunting* in the Stronghold!"

Dither was finding it harder to keep the bile out of her tone, but she kept smiling.

"I have a permit!" Aldonas hissed.

Lightning flashed across the sky, tearing the clouds apart with a thunder clap that sent torrents of rain down on them.

"I, um . . . " said Grover, red-faced and panting, backing away.

"Don't worry about old Professor Angry-Face over there," said Dither, casually smiling up at him. "Tell me about yourself! Why have you decided to join the park-keepers? Isn't the Academy challenging enough for you?"

"It's . . . well . . . " Grover stammered.

"Dither." Aldonas was looming at her side again. "Why don't we find your dress and leave these people to their work?"

We? Dither ground her teeth. *Now there's a "we". There wasn't a "we" when I was longing for him for years. There wasn't a "we" after he initiated a sexual encounter in the live oak grove. And there won't be a "we" as soon as he's bonded to some other woman at the Valentine's Feast.*

"Just a moment," she waved him away, smiling even as fury churned in her gut and desperation stung her eyes. "I'm trying to get to know one of Th'myskôra's fine young people." Her hair was saturated, plastered flat against her head and bare shoulders, rivulets of rainwater leaking down her back and breasts. Her nipples tightened to tiny daggers under the freezing water.

"Will you at least cover up?" Aldonas wrapped one wing around her.

"I don't think I will!" Dither said, stepping out into view, fingers tightening around her rock. "Well? Grover?"

"It's . . . you . . . I just . . . " Grover's gaze fell to Dither's breasts. She saw him look. Aldonas saw him look. Everyone saw him look. "I think I saw a dress over there!" Before anyone else could speak, young Grover Gribble was at the edge of the fairgrounds, looking very intently at some muddy scrub brush and nothing else.

"You're making everyone uncomfortable," Aldonas hissed, trying once again to cover her with his wing.

"Am I?" asked Dither, pressing the pointed tip of her cock-playing rock into her own chest. "Am *I* making *everyone* uncomfortable? Pytr! Am I making you uncomfortable?"

"Not in the slightest," Pytr said, grinning broadly at her.

Lightning struck again, and a terrible wind howled through the fairgrounds.

"*You* stay out of this!" Aldonas shouted over the wind.

"It seems a little unreasonable of you to expect a private conversation out here in public," said the human, arching a brow soberly.

"I think," shouted Dither, jumping into a nearby mud puddle, "that *you're* the only one who's uncomfortable." She scooped up a big handful of thick mud and smeared it all over her naked body. "I, for one, have never been *more* comfortable than I am right now!"

"Dither," Aldonas had his wing spread again, trying to cover her. "Please control yourself."

"No!" she barked. The wind intensified, sending hard rain flying horizontally into their faces, obscuring the tears sneaking down her cheeks. "You control yourself! *I'm* a child of the woods!" Dither ran around him as fast as she could, making thick, wet circles in the mud. "I am chaos manifest!"

The work crew was all doubled over. "It looks like *you're* the one getting a lesson today, *professor,*" Pytr howled with laughter.

"Stop running," Aldonas commanded.

"Or what?" Dither goaded, her squeaky voice cracking. "You'll chase me?" She scooped up a handful of mud and pelted him, still circling, still clutching her rock.

"Dither, I'm warning you."

Rain burned her eyes, but it was nothing compared to the sting of being Aldonas' on-again, off-again plaything.

"And what if you catch me? Huh? You don't want me — *that's* clear!"

"I would really like to discuss this in private."

"He wants to discuss *this* in private!" she called to the group of park-keepers, her heart twisting in her tiny chest. "You know what he didn't bother discussing in private?"

"What?" asked a cyclops between giggles.

"Birth control!" Dither shouted, still running, still throwing wet clumps of earth at Aldonas through the pounding rain.

He flinched every time a cold little mud ball hit him, but he kept his head pointed rigidly forward. He refused to turn.

"For all *he* knows, I'm pregnant right now."

"I . . . I didn't think that was possible," Aldonas said, giving the first indication of emotion since their audience arrived.

"You didn't *think*? That seems kind of important to me. Sort of like one of those things you should be sure about before you let loose your seed inside a person, don't you think?"

"Please," Aldonas said, "control yourself."

"No," Dither shouted. "I *won't* control myself." She remembered the flat rock in her hand, the one she'd used to tame him the night before. "And I won't control *your*self anymore, either!" She threw the rock, hitting him square in the chest. Aldonas didn't flinch.

I can't even throw a stupid rock hard enough to hurt him.

"That isn't fair." Aldonas looked down at the rock as it splashed unceremoniously in the mud.

"Why *are* you so obsessed with self-control anyway?" Dither demanded.

"Because," Aldonas bellowed, cool façade finally cracking, "someone could get hurt!"

Dither stopped. She stared up into his eyes, searching for some clue that he felt anything for her besides embarrassment.

"This is me!" she squeaked, not bothering to sniffle as snot leaked out of her nose. "I love mud, and I hate clothes! I collect snails and commune with toadstools and, yes, sometimes, on occasion, I take things without permission."

"Sometimes?" Aldonas quirked his head.

"Fine!" Dither stomped her little foot. "I love stealing! I'm a goblin!"

"Hear, hear!" shouted Pytr and his crew.

"Maybe that means I'm not good enough for you — but at least *I'm* honest. I'm not trying to cover up what I am!"

"Dither," Aldonas stepped toward her, opening his wings again, "I never . . . not for one second—"
"Except you did!" Dither shouted. "Ever since I came to work at the Academy, you've been telling me I wasn't good enough for you."

"I never said—"

"But you knew! You knew I was interested in you the whole time. Admit it!" The wind whipped Dither's wet hair across her face.

"I knew," Aldonas looked down at the rock in the mud.

"You knew! And you told me again and again *for years* that you couldn't stand to look at me."

"I never said that," Aldonas pleaded.

"No!" Dither snapped. "You said, 'Get away from me, flee while you can!'"

"Dither, you don't understand."

"And I got away!" Her heart raced, her ears burned, and her numb finger trembled as she poked it in his dripping feathers. "Every time you rejected me, I did exactly what you wanted, didn't I?"

"Yes," Aldonas clicked his beak and quirked his head from one side to the other.

"I stayed away from you and convinced myself to get over you, and the second I felt like I'd moved on, *there* you'd be, following me around, pulling me back in! You're . . . you're like a cat playing with the mouse it caught!"

"Dither, it's not like that," Aldonas insisted. "Just calm down and —"

"What *is* it like, Aldonas?" Her eyes were puffy and red — no amount of rain could hide the fact that she was crying now. "I'm good enough to fuck when no one's around, but not good enough to be seen with in public?"

"We were seen together literally all day yesterday."

"Yeah," she stomped. "By all the other women, who are *not* me, that you're considering bonding to!"

"This whole thing was *your* idea," Aldonas shouted.

"*My* idea?" Dither was so angry she could barely stand to look at him. "You *volunteered*!"

"Only because I wanted to help you," Aldonas rolled his eyes. "*I* don't care about Jack Valentine!"

"You *take that back*." Dither's gaze narrowed. The wind whipped in her ears.

The park-keepers fell silent.

Aldonas stood inert.

"Excuse me, professor?" Grover had returned with a dripping bundle of wool and cotton. "I found your girlfriend's things."

"She's *not* my girlfriend!" Aldonas bawked, much too quickly.

Hot tears spilled down Dither's cheeks, and she snatched her ruined clothes. "I may be a goblin, Aldonas Strigidae, but at least I'm not a liar!"

CHAPTER 11

ALDONAS

"Dither," Aldonas took a steadying breath, his talons scraping along the path between Academy housing and the main campus. "I'm not happy with the way things ended on the fairgrounds yesterday."

It was raining again. It had rained so hard the night before that Aldonas had a fitful, restless sleep. It was definitely the weather that kept him up, *not* his worrying about Dither.

He hadn't bothered to bring his cloak; it was still caked with mud anyway.

"I'm sure we both said and did things that we regret, and I would like to express my most sincere apology for intimating that you weren't... that I don't want . . . that you aren't my—"

"Muttering to yourself, Mr. Strigidae?" asked old Professor Oloborous as he trundled past.

"Oh, no, sir!" Aldonas stammered. "I was just . . . practicing my lecture. My introduction to blood magic class is going to attempt the low stone spell today."

"Good man!" called the elderly arachnid, the fleshy tips of his six segmented legs thudding against the wet cobblestone. "One can never be too precise with one's words. You know the old saying: 'Sloppy syntax sabotages success!'"

Inside the Academy, the grand stone staircase was treacherous, as it always was on rainy days. Aldonas gripped the handrail tightly as his talons threatened to skid out from under him.

"Surely," he muttered under his breath, "you must see the utility in maintaining a level of respectability?" Yesterday, he'd let emotion control his behavior; he'd been too upset to present his arguments clearly. Now, he pictured Dither quite clearly in his mind's eye: listening intently, nodding along, easily and immediately convinced by his dispassionate logic.

"I'm not asking you to change your entire personality, Dither, but when people care deeply for each other . . . that is, if you'll just control a few of your . . . less acceptable urges, I'm sure you'll find yourself moving through life much more easily."

Aldonas reached the third-story landing. Soon he'd arrive at the lecture hall, and Dither would be there with the supply cart.

"I'll lay out my case, just like that, and then she and I will have a spirited debate which will end as soon as I present her with my shining cock, and everything can go back to the way it was."

But when Aldonas reached his door, his heart sank; there was no haughty green goblin there to meet him. Just her wooden cart, its contents carefully alphabetized and labeled: abalone shells, barley flour, lances, narwhal pestles, tiger beetles, unicorn tears, and dried woundwarts. And something else — a small cotton sack, tied at the top and attached to a large, folded piece of parchment. Aldonas removed every hint of despair from his face and wheeled the cart inside.

"Good morning, professor!" chirped Briar, a bright cyclops girl and the first student to arrive. "Would you like some help passing out today's supplies?"

Aldonas ran a wing over the cart, hiding Dither's surprise in his feathers. "Thank you, Briar. That would be very helpful."

As more students filtered into the hall, Aldonas surreptitiously weighed the strange little package in his wing.

What could she have left for me? After yesterday's fight, I wouldn't have thought she'd be giving me anything . . . Knowing Dither, it could just as easily be a snail as a cursed poppet.

"Professor?"

Who am I kidding? After the way I behaved yesterday, she wouldn't waste a snail on me.

"Professor?" asked Kreston Quaff.

Aldonas looked up and noticed for the first time fifty-two puzzled faces staring down at him.

Make that fifty-one.

"Mr. Quaff," he said, turning his huge yellow eyes on the siren in the last row. "Where is Mr. Gribble?" The memory of the jittery were-vole ogling Dither's bare breasts flashed across his mind.

"He stayed home, professor; he wasn't feeling well."

He'd be feeling a far sight worse if I didn't prize self-control so highly. I'll be sure to point that out when I finally find Dither.

"In his absence, Mr. Quaff, it falls to you. Please remind the class of today's objective."

"We're casting the low stone spell," said Kreston. "The objective is to try and call a small item into our experience."

"Close!" declared Aldonas. "Unfortunately, when practicing blood magic, close is not good enough. Can anyone help Mr. Quaff?"

Half a dozen hands shot up around the room.

"Miss Seathrift?"

A tall, ruddy human girl answered, "He said 'try.' Trying indicates doubt, and blood magic will only work if applied with absolute certainty."

"Very good, Miss Seathrift. It is not enough to *mearly* want a thing, to hope for it, or to try for it. We must *know* that it is so. It is only in the knowing that we are able to bend reality to our will." Aldonas felt Dither's note under his wing.

She has forgiven me. She is willing to see my side of the argument, and she's given up on trying to find my "true love match."

He repeated the words in his head, but he didn't believe them.

"Who can tell us the procedure? Mr. Deathstroggle?"

"Yes, sir. First, we add three spoonfuls of barley flour to the abalone bowl . . ."

The tiefling kept speaking, explaining the day's assignment perfectly, Aldonas assumed. He couldn't force himself to focus on anything other than the contents of Dither's note.

"And then you say, 'Oh, little thing, tiny joy, come into my life. 'Tis long that I have yearned for you to turn my darkness bright.' And that's it."

"Alright, get started, everyone." Aldonas sat behind his desk while the class worked. For a while, he pretended to grade papers while his mind wandered back to Dither.

What did she write? What could Dither Weaselsnout possibly be too embarrassed to say in person? She could be apologizing for embarrassing me in front of those workers yesterday. A woman like that probably isn't used to apologizing . . . For all I know, this is her first time!

He looked up at his class. Most of them seemed about halfway through adding ingredients.

I shouldn't have chosen such a complicated spell. Blood and Bile wouldn't have taken half this long.

And all that time, Dither's letter sat, sealed and unread, on the edge of his desk.

Who am I kidding? Dither hasn't written me an apology. That note is probably four pages long and overflowing with her favorite swamp-related curse words. As dramatic as she is, I wouldn't be surprised if she challenged me to a duel. I'll probably have to meet her at sundown and wrestle a poisoned spear out of her hands before she'll even consider talking things through.

"Oh, little thing, tiny joy, come into my life. 'Tis long that I have yearned for you to turn my darkness bright." A few voices chanted the incantation asynchronously, then a few more.

Aldonas could practically hear Dither's note screaming his name.

Just a few more minutes, and I'll be alone; then I can finally read that damnable letter.

Finally, the last student was done.

"Excellent work today, class. I'm going to let you leave early, but don't forget the examination on Wednesday."

"An exam?" someone groaned, prolonging Aldonas' agonizing wait.

"Exactly as promised at the beginning of the term." Aldonas clacked his beak. "Closed book. Closed note. Cumulative. If you've been paying attention, it shouldn't take more than an hour or so."

"But, professor," whined Kreston Quaff while Dither's note sat, unread, on the desk. "The Valentine's Feast is tomorrow. No one wants to spend all day studying."

"Your *education* is for life, Mr. Quaff, if *you* don't prioritize it, no one will."

The moment the last student left the room, Aldonas bolted the door behind them. He grabbed Dither's letter and sliced open the wax seal.

Aldonas,

I have prepared your supplies as previously discussed. Please have all future acquisition requests pinned to your door at the end of each week. If you do not submit your requests in writing, they will not be fulfilled.

Do not, under any circumstances, follow me around the island or make contact with me in any way. I no longer wish to know you.

If you have one honest bone in your body, you will fulfill your promise to help me satisfy Jack Valentine. I've enclosed an enchanted copper key.

Aldonas untied the little pouch and turned it upside down. An ornate copper key clattered out onto his desk.

Take it with you to the pleasure pit at the Valentine's Feast tomorrow night. Your match will be waiting with a corresponding lock. Don't worry — she will be an expert in fitting in, just like you. She'll be a match you will be proud to be seen in public with.

If you have any respect for me at all, you'll keep your word.

Aldonas sank back into his chair. "She didn't even bother cursing me. A fight I could handle, but indifference? Is she just going to hide from me for the rest of our lives on this tiny island? Working in the same building? I can't believe that the same woman who looked at me with so much passion and devotion burning in her eyes is willing to give up on me — give up on *us* — as soon as we have one fight!"

Aldonas stomped angrily around the room. "Infernal goblin logic! She'll find my mate, will she? And I'm just supposed to go along with whatever decision she and Jack Valentine make about *my* life? Well, I say that Dither Weaselsnout can't find my true love match — because I've already found her!"

He shoved the key into his pocket and stormed out of the room. "And it's about time I give my one, true love match a piece of my mind." He reached the door to the service stairs and barreled through it. "No one is going to tell me what I can't do, and that includes Dither Weaselsnout!"

He lumbered down the narrow wooden staircase, shouting

all the way. "And another thing!" He reached the second-story landing. "*If* there were any chance that some other woman was my love match, do you really think I would have spent the last two terms struggling not to eat *you*!"

First story landing. "How can someone who is so clever understand so little about relationships?" Aldonas finally stood at Dither's dimly lit basement door. He pounded on it.

"Dither, come out here and talk to me!"

There was no answer.

He pounded again.

"Dither, if you think I'm going to bond to some other woman just because we had a fight, you're insane! That's not how love works!"

Dither still didn't answer, and Aldonas kept banging his wing against her door. He was considering knocking it down when a small, crumpled piece of parchment fell from the crack between the door and its frame.

The Academy storeroom will be closed for the rest of the week due to a religious observance.

Jack Valentine must be satisfied!

CHAPTER 12

DITHER

The morning rain had stopped, and the evening rain hadn't yet begun as Dither stood in an ornate oak entryway, wearing her last intact woolen dress. She'd asked Jack Valentine for guidance, and the burning in her bosom had brought her to this exact spot.

She stood with a human woman beneath the new wooden sign that read *Mimple's Toy Shoppe* and creaked on its hinges in the wind. There was no doubt in Dither's mind that the tall, prim-looking human — with her thick hair braided neatly under a caul and veil — was a potential true love match for Aldonas.

"And you're saying all I have to do is show up at the festival with this lock tomorrow, and that tall, good-looking birdman will marry me?" asked Elisabetta, the buxom, auburn-haired toymaker holding a small chisel and a block of wood.

"That's right!" Dither proclaimed through her tightest smile. It was all taking much too long.

"And what do *you* get out of this?" she said, turning the lock over suspiciously in her hand.

How is it so difficult to convince someone to be loved forever?

Dither sighed. "I am a devotee of Jack Valentine." She placed her hand solemnly over her heart. "It is my sacred duty to bring together true love matches, *especially* on Valentine's Day! The holiest day of the year!"

It didn't matter if her heart ached at the thought of handing Aldonas over to another match. It didn't matter how cruel his words had been to her. Dither had her devotion to Jack Valentine, and her duty brought her clarity through the haze of her own despair. Elisabetta was indeed a suitable match for Aldonas; all that was left was to convince both parties to let love happen to them.

"Hmmm . . . " Elisabetta sucked her plump, pink lower lip between her teeth. "I've been warned about accepting gifts from goblins, and a whole husband is a pretty big gift. How do I know this isn't some sort of trick?"

Dither refused to roll her eyes. *How's* that *for self-control?*

The only "trick" was the one Aldonas had played on her by pretending to be interested.

"Jack Valentine will only be satisfied if it's a true love match!" Dither explained, forcing herself to smile with fake cheer. "No goblin would *dream* of playing such a trick!"

"Alright," the human laughed warmly. "You've convinced me. I'll give your professor a shot."

"Not *my* professor!" Dither cried. "He's your professor now."

"Not right now, though?" the human asked. "I do still get to meet him first, don't I?"

"Of course," said Dither. "Just don't take too long deciding. Once you do, the binding magic will only work during golden hour tomorrow."

"And if I don't like him, I can leave? There's no love potion being used?"

"If you don't like him, you can leave. But you *will* like him. Jack Valentine has indicated that a very strong physical attraction exists between you, as well as the necessary compatibilities for long-term happiness."

The human squinted down at Dither for several long seconds. "Alright. I'll be there tomorrow," she finally said.

"Yes! Yes, this is wonderful," said Dither, bouncing up and down on her toes. "You won't regret it!" She hurried out of the little toy shop, back to the safety of the grey, misty street.

Outside, evidence of the impending festivities was everywhere. Creatures big and small had already begun donning their most titillating red and pink attire. Shop windows were full to bursting with pennants and banners. And everywhere Dither turned, some happy couple was canoodling.

"Those park-keepers sure work fast," she muttered, peering into the fairgrounds at the pleasure pit where a sprawling, shimmering red tent, open at its apex, had already been erected. She could hear workers moving around underneath, reinforcing the moat and testing the drain.

"Junction six should be clear now," called a distant voice. "Send another load through!"

"How romantic." Dither gritted her teeth.

Smaller tents were going up all over the fairgrounds. Creatures hoping to trade mead, ale, jewelry, love potions, and magical marital aids flooded the island from across the Three Realms. Tomorrow, there'd even be creatures performing quickie marriages filling the area.

"There'll be something for everyone," Dither muttered, flicking her foot through a mud puddle.

Glass lanterns blown into the shape of Valentine's hearts were stationed every few feet, hung from iron posts. At night, they would flicker to life with soft mood lighting that would bathe the entire fairground in a romantic, pinkish glow.

Dither splashed down Zeluk Row, determined to get home as soon as possible; she'd had quite enough merriment. Unfortunately, she couldn't ignore the large, vibrant pink and red roses, hydrangeas, dahlias, and peonies blooming *everywhere* — on bushes, through cracks in the cobbles, on the sides of buildings ... There was at least one devastatingly perfect flower growing unnaturally on every surface, in every direction.

"Perfect," Dither grumbled. "It's all frogging perfect!"

"Just wait until tomorrow," squeaked a minuscule voice from a nearby peony. It was Parvi Florum, standing with her little hands on her hips, admiring her own work. "When the sun goes down, all of these enchanted blooms are going to glow pink!"

"That sounds lovely," Dither sniffled. "But I won't be here to see it."

"What do you mean?" asked Parvi. Despite her cherubic face and adorable little flower petal dress, she spoke with loving authority. She was the oldest Eldrich on the island, maybe the oldest in all the Realms. Parvi Florum was *the* default auntie to every creature who moved into Th'myskôra's enchanted woods. "I heard you with that human; don't you want to watch her love match turn his key in her lock? Who are you setting her up with anyway?"

"Aldonas," Dither admitted, sniffling.

"The strix? The one you had that big, naked blowout with yesterday?"

"You heard about that, huh?"

"I'm a pixie, darling. I hear about everything."

"The human will be a good match for him. They're both similarly . . . buttoned up."

"It sounds like you and your boyfriend got into your first fight, and now you're trying to foist him off onto another girl."

"No! That's . . . no!" Dither stammered. "Aldonas was never my boyfriend, and yesterday he made that very clear."

"Maybe he just needs a little time adjusting to the idea; those buttoned-up types often require a good deal of patience."

"I'm all out of patience for Aldonas the strix." Dither began to cry. It was impossible not to when Parvi was looking up at her with all of that knowing, maternal concern on her face. "He's been leading me on for *years*. And I'm not going to allow it anymore! He can wilt someone else's mycelium from now on!"

"Liar," Parvi said playfully, her tiny voice tinkling. She flew up to Dither's shoulder and landed there, tapping her foot impatiently. "You're not done with that strix at all. In fact," she lowered her voice, "you've fallen in love with him."

Dither opened her mouth to mount a defense. "I made a mistake . . . Well, actually, a series of mistakes. Extremely erotic mistakes, but now it's time to erase those mistakes."

Parvi's tiny hand flew up. "I know when a goblin is in love . . . I also happen to know a thing or three about the mating habits of the strix. If you let him bond to that human woman, you'll regret it for the rest of your life."

"Don't *you* start too." Dither's throat tightened. "Aldonas doesn't love me. How could he?" Dither dabbed her dripping nose with her huge bell sleeve. "It doesn't matter — as long as Jack Valentine is satisfied, I'll be fine."

"I *knew* Jack Valentine," the tiny sprite scolded. "He would not want you to sacrifice your heart's desire!"

"Jack Valentine demands true love matches!" Dither protested. "Aldonas and this human are a match."

"Is she his *only* potential love match on the island?" The tiny pixie stared daggers at Dither. "Is that what you're telling me?"

"I don't know," Dither sniffled. "That is, I didn't ask."

"You didn't think to ask if *you* might be a match to him?"

"I'm just a goblin," Dither whimpered. "And he's so . . . he's so . . ."

"Oh, you silly girl . . . It's not for you to decide who is and isn't worthy of love. Let Jack Valentine make the matches!"

"No!" Dither squeaked. "I'm *done* planning and plotting how to win over Aldonas the strix. I've spent too long already trying to trick him into wanting me, and the only person I ended up tricking was myself. From now on, I'm through with love, and the sooner Aldonas is partnered off with that human woman, the sooner I'll be free."

Dither spun on her heel, launching Parvi through the air, and ran the rest of the way home.

ALDONAS

Aldonas sat alone in his lecture hall. The perfect symmetry of the gleaming sandstone bricks that formed the rotunda seemed unnecessary, almost offensive, to him now. Dither's note was gripped in his wing. *I no longer wish to know you.*

"That's ... that's so final ..."

Outside, the sun was setting. Lanterns around the room flickered magically to life. There was no reason for Aldonas to still be on campus ... no reason other than that he didn't know where to go when he wasn't following Dither.

"How did I let things get so out of hand?" The memory of Dither's furious little mud-streaked face gnawed at his memory. "She was crying." Aldonas smoothed out the parchment, revealing Dither's shaky scrawl. "She was sobbing, and I just stood there."

He paced slowly between the rows of student desks, moving

up towards the large, arched windows at the back of the class-room. With each step, his talons sank ever so slightly into the soft wooden floorboards. Aldonas remembered the feeling of splintering the wooden barrel as he'd dived, talons first, at Dither. "I could have killed her, but Dither was never afraid of me, not really. She's either incredibly brave or entirely too trusting."

He sighed and leaned his forehead against the cold glass. "One thing's for certain — I'm a coward. A coward and a liar. Dither was right: I've spent my whole life trying to hide what I am. And now I've ruined my one chance at happiness, at really being understood."

"Practicing another lecture, Mr. Strigidae?" asked old Professor Oloborous, poking his round, grey head in the room. "Don't work too late; a young man like you will want to rest up tonight."

Aldonas crumpled the note and shoved it into his pocket. "I'm not sure I understand your meaning."

"Oh, come now!" The rotund arachnid let himself into the room and made himself right at home behind Aldonas' oak desk. "Tomorrow is the Valentine's Feast! You don't mean to tell me that there's *no one* on the island you're hoping to find in the pleasure pit!"

"The pleasure pit?" Aldonas blushed. He hurried back down to his desk and began hastily shoving papers into his satchel — anything to look busy, to stop the old man from asking about Valentine's Day. "I, uh . . . I wouldn't know anything about that.

I was, uh … planning on catching up on some grading tomorrow."

"What a pity." Professor Oloborous shook his head and clicked his mouth parts thoughtfully. "I suppose it's true what they say: young men are rarely smart enough to wield their powerful loins appropriately."

"I'm not sure I'm familiar with that aphorism," Aldonas said, stepping out into the hallway. "I'd better get home, it's getting dark."

"Oh, good!" said the old spider, following Aldonas down the grand staircase. "I'm on my way back to Academy housing myself! We can walk together."

Aldonas did not want to walk home with Professor Oloborous. He wanted some more time to wallow alone. Maybe he could even find Dither and talk it out with her.

If I don't show up to . . . "satisfy Jack Valentine" tomorrow, she'll never forgive me. Either I bond to a woman I don't even know, let alone love, and I lose Dither forever — or I refuse to show up and still lose her.

"Now, I've always said what staff members do in their out-of-office hours is their own business, but it is a minute island, and word gets around . . ."

"What?" Aldonas only just realized that his old mentor had been speaking to him for several minutes.

"Don't misunderstand me, boy," the giant spider said, stepping down the Academy's front steps and onto the cobblestone path. "I'm no prude, far from it. I only want to know … how did you do it?"

"Do what?"

"Suppress the urge to hunt, of course! Come, man, everyone knows that goblins are a natural food source for strixes!"

"Everyone?" Aldonas had not known that; admittedly, he didn't know much about his own people. His parents had tried very hard to raise him in the human way, insisting that he sleep in a bed and eat cooked food from a plate. They never hunted as a family or spoke the strix language at home. He wasn't sure he'd ever even seen his father transform.

"Well, maybe not *everyone*," the sly old man admitted. "But those of us who still remember the old ways do."

"There seems to be a growing trend of younger people reviving the old ways," Aldonas said, remembering Dither's collection of ancient tomes and long-buried treasures.

"That's refreshing to know!" cried the old man, several of his beady eyes gleaming.

Aldonas had never given the old ways much thought. He'd been hatched the same year the War ended, and his parents had always said he was their key to the future. They raised him to seek out the latest innovations, to learn the ins and outs of all the newest treaties. "No son of mine is going to be caught standing still while the world moves on around him," his mother always said when his grandmother tried to intervene in his education. Aldonas had always prided himself on living on the leading edge.

Perhaps there is some wisdom in those old children's stories after all . . .

"There is a certain woman, you see," Professor Oloborous said, clicking his mouthparts and tenting his fingers, "whom I would very much like to get to know better. But when I'm alone with her, I'm overwhelmed by an urge to trap her tiny, fluttering wings in a deadly web! Exsanguination is not especially romantic . . ."

"No, I don't suppose it is."

"So? How did you do it? How do you stop yourself from hunting Dither?"

"I . . ." Aldonas looked at the live oak grove where he'd first touched her all those months ago. If he closed his eyes, he could conjure the smell of crushed mint leaves at the bottom of the hill where he'd first filled her with his seed. "I didn't stop hunting her," he said. "She stopped running."

"Well," the old man sighed, "I don't know how much that's going to help me snare a particularly perky pixie, but it does give me some comfort knowing that at least one predator on this island has found true love with his prey."

"I . . . I hate to disillusion you, professor, but —"

"In the old days, such a match would never even be considered! There may be hope for this elderly arachnid after all."

"That's just it," Aldonas said. "I drove her away. She doesn't want to see me anymore."

"Well, you aren't going to give up, are you?"

"She was pretty clear, professor. She said never to contact her again — that she didn't want to know me anymore. She's even insisting that I bond to another woman tomorrow at the Valentine's Feast."

"No one can force a love bond, son," the old man said thoughtfully. "If the participants aren't truly in love with one another, the magic won't stick."

"Well, Dither seems to think it will . . . According to her, as long as there's potential for a match, Jack Valentine will handle the rest."

"Jack Valentine, eh?" Professor Oloborous scratched his chin. "He's a trickster sprite, isn't he? Nothing's ever that straightforward with Jack Valentine."

"Well, he's certainly played a trick on me — if he's real, that is." The two men turned off the cobblestone street and headed up the little incline toward the large apartment building maintained by the Academy for its students and staff. "Why bring Dither into my life? Why make her irresistible to me if I'm not allowed to keep her?"

"Maybe you haven't earned her yet," the old spider mused. "In the old days, courting males performed grand gestures to win the favors of their ladies fair . . ."

"That would be a trick, since Dither has decided to hide from me for the rest of our lives."

"Don't be so sullen, my boy," Professor Oloborous said, slapping him on the back. "It hinders creativity. Why, in the old days, we would perform elaborate dances, and build ornate webs, and steal precious jewels, and fight duels to the death, and—"

"Precious jewels? I think Dither would rather receive an interesting rock than a ruby ..." Aldonas stopped in his tracks. "That's it! Professor, can you tell me anything about Jack Valentine?"

The old man chuckled. "I'm not *that* old!"

"I mean, how was he worshipped? In the old days, how would people honor him? Dither said she found the *most* appropriate ritual for the island, which must mean there are other rituals!"

"Well, yes," Professor Oloborous mumbled. "I seem to remember his devotees having an affinity for the back door . . . I believe I have an ancient courting scroll in my apartment that outlines the necessary steps."

"Perfect!" Aldonas grabbed Professor Oloborous by the arm and dragged him hurriedly toward Academy housing. "Tell me everything you know about goblins' back doors!"

CHAPTER 14

DITHER

Dither lay face down in her goblin nest — a heaping collection of mismatched down-stuffed pillows, nestled in the deepest part of her earthen den.

"Happy frogging Valentine's Day," she grumbled for at least the fourteenth time that day. Outside, she could hear sprites, brownies, and nymphs all giggling and scampering from olive tree to oak to ash, along muddied paths and streams, through soggy yellow leaf litter. She hadn't even bothered getting out of her sleeping gown, and she hadn't had a proper meal all day. Every leaf of the Eldrich Forest was teeming with erotic energy, and try as she might, Dither couldn't ignore it.

"Bellindelle," said a husky male voice outside her window. "I can't keep my feelings a secret from you any longer."

"Oh?" a female voice teased. "Was *that* what you call 'keeping a secret'?"

Then there was a thud followed by sounds of kissing and moaning as the eager young couple collided into each other and into Dither's tree trunk, shaking the whole den.

"A girl can't even *wallow* in peace!" Dither rolled out of her nest and landed with a thud on the floor. "Get out of here, you canoodlers!" She grabbed a broom and banged it against the glass until the frisky young brownie removed her backside from Dither's window, and the noisy lovers scampered off, giggling as they went.

"It's just one day," Dither told herself, rubbing her temple. "Everyone is going to go right back to normal as soon as the decorations come down and the ale wears off." She considered getting back in her nest, where she'd been lying all day. "What's the use? I couldn't sleep anymore today if a basilisk kissed me!"

More voices floated in, interrupting her peace. "You don't really think she's going to go through with it, do you?" asked a gnome walking by.

"Humans aren't exactly known for keeping their word," said a pixie, "but she'd be a fool to turn down a match like *that*. I mean, they have practically *no* magical abilities — they can't even call fruits and vegetables up from the earth at will."

"It's a wonder they manage to feed themselves at all," laughed the gnome.

"Lucky for her, strixes hunt for their *own* food!"

"And take it raw!" The two women filtered out of earshot,

laughing and gossiping, no doubt on their way to the pleasure pit.

"Today is the last day you'll ever have to think of Aldonas the strix," Dither soothed heraching heart. "By sundown, he'll be bonded to that human, and you can go on with your life."

She dragged herself up the little wooden staircase to the den's main chamber, a spacious hole dug half in the earth, and half in the center of a huge tree stump.

"Maybe mulled wine will make me feel better."

Dither threw a fresh log onto the cooking fire and dipped a ladle into the small cast-iron cauldron that hung over the flame. She filled a tankard and raised it to no one.

"Happy Valentine's Day!" She drank deeply, letting the heady, familiar blend of spices and alcohol rush down her throat. "All hail Jack Valentine!" she cheered, alone in her den on what should have been the best day of the year. Try as she might, she couldn't get Parvi's words out of her head.

Maybe I do have a true love match living on Th'myskôra after all. It sure would take some of the sting out of losing Aldonas...

Dither pressed her little nose to a window and looked at revelers, all dressed in their finest red gowns and pink tunics — rushing, hands clasped, towards the fairgrounds.

You didn't lose him because you never had *him. Aldonas never once held your hand, or took you to a festival, or asked you to go on a date with him.*

Dither wrapped a blanket around her shoulders and got another tankard of wine before settling into the very large hip-joint armchair she'd gotten from an ogre.

"I wonder if Aldonas is there yet . . . wonder if he'll make small talk with the human first, or just slide his key right in."

This isn't helpful, Dither. You should make some dinner or something . . .

Before Dither could settle her argument with herself, she was interrupted by something scratching at her back door.

"No one's home!" she called out, pulling the blanket up over her head.

The scratching persisted.

"Normally, I'm a big fan of both mischief *and* foolishness," she shouted, "but right now, I'd really like to be alone, thank you!"

More scratching.

"I said, *get!*" Dither marched across the room and flung open the door. But no one was there — only a large wooden crate. "Gifts? At my back door on Valentine's Day? Only an acolyte of Jack Valentine would know this ancient custom."

She pried off the lid and pulled out the contents one by one. A shining pewter spoon from the Saffron Smile, three shimmering slipper shells, a sachet filled with dried mint, a skein of chimera yarn, a purple sea-otter vertebra, and the same flat, jagged rock she'd bashed against Aldonas' cock that evening in the pleasure pit.

"Is this all . . . for me?" At the bottom of the crate was a brand-new silk gown. It was a shimmery, pastel pink, and along the hem and the scalloped edges of the bell sleeves, copper-colored keys and locks had been embroidered with glittering thread.

Dither held the gown up to her tiny frame, admiring the tight bodice and elegant sweeping neckline. "I've got to try you on!" She pulled off the woolen blanket and stepped into her new gown. When she slid her arm through its sleeve, a small piece of parchment floated to the floor.

Each of us has dozens of potential love matches throughout the Realms.

Consult Jack Valentine — if he wills it, meet me at the entrance of the pleasure pit at sundown.

"By the spirit of Jack Valentine," Dither rasped, clutching the note to her chest. Even after Parvi Florum's lecture, she hadn't let herself imagine that she had a true love match waiting for her — not really. She took Aldonas' rejections at face value, and it hurt, but it was the kind of heartbreak she could manage. She'd never dared summon the power of mischief within herself, never dared to ask Jack Valentine to make *her* a match.

"What if I don't have one?" She paced across the room. "What if I'm destined to live my life alone, serving Jack Valentine by making love matches for others, but never knowing it myself?"

A creeping fear crawled up the back of her neck, and a premature grief churned her stomach. "What if Aldonas sent me the crate? What if he didn't? What if some other creature is my true love match?"

That was it — her real fear, the thing she hadn't been brave enough to even think before. "If my true love match is someone else, then everything I thought I felt for Aldonas was . . . a lie. How will I ever trust myself again if Jack Valentine confirms that Aldonas and I were never meant to be?"

Dither looked again at the treasures assembled in the crate. "No one but Aldonas could have gathered these specific gifts. If he was bold enough to drag this crate across the island and talk some sprite into scratching at my back door, I suppose I can be brave enough to face the truth."

Dither took a steadying breath and placed her hands over her heart. "Oh, great Jack Valentine," she prayed, voice trembling. "Are Aldonas and I a true love match? Should I go to the feast?"

She held her breath, stomach churning, skin clammy. For a long time, there was no answer...

And then, a prickling warmth rushed through her. Joy and certainty like she'd never felt before filled her body so completely that there could be no doubt: Jack Valentine had meant Aldonas to be her match all along…

…and she had paired him up with another woman!

"I have to get to the fairground!"

Dither dragged the box inside, ran to the wash basin, and scrubbed her face, the new gown still just half on. She braided her wild green hair and accentuated the complicated plaits with several shiny lizard teeth.

"How foolish of me, trying to skip the feast," she moaned. If she were truly to honor Jack Valentine, she must add to the island's collective spirit of romantic love personally.

She mashed some cloudberries and spread their juices across her cheeks, adding a subtle, rosy hue to their apples. "I should have seen it before! *Of course,* Jack Valentine has sent me a match who is a puzzle! There's no mischief in a straightfor-ward romance."

Dither fastened the tiny buttons that ran the length of her bodice and stood in front of her polished brass mirror. "Beauti-ful," she squeaked, looking at her own reflection with newfound appreciation. Something was missing, though…

"Of course!" Dither rushed outside and hurried back to the mirror with an upturned snail in her hand. She pressed the snail's foot to her lips and slid it back and forth, ensuring an even application of slime. "Now *that's* how you satisfy Jack Valentine!"

The sky was darkening outside her window. "Bog flogit! It's nearly sunset *now*!"

CHAPTER 15

DITHER

"Don't . . . open her . . . lock," Dither panted, holding a burning stitch in her side. She'd arrived just as the sun was sinking below the horizon. "Did I miss it? Am I too late?" Dither made it to the pleasure pit, an expansive, round, red tent whose pointed roof was left open so that revelers' unions would be blessed by both the sun's rays and the glowing moon.

"You're exactly on time," cooed a familiar voice.

Dither spun around. "Aldonas? So that *was* you at the back door with the trinkets?" She beamed at him. "But how did you get past the barrier?"

"It wasn't so difficult, once I asked for a little help . . . " His face pulled up to one side in the closest thing to a smile that a person without lips could manage. "I have another gift for you, Dither." Aldonas reached back to his tail and pulled out one perfect, spotted brown feather and handed it to her.

She held it gently, tracing a finger carefully along its edge. "But . . . " Dither's lip trembled. "But you said the power of a strix's feather is too great! You said it wasn't safe to just hand them out to anybody."

"You aren't just anybody," Aldonas said, wrapping Dither's hand around his impossibly soft feather. "You're my mate. Everything I have is yours to wield, including this magic."

"I'm your . . . ? But you . . . ?" Dither shook her head, confused. "This is a lot. Two days ago, you didn't even want me to be your girlfriend... And now you're . . . I'm not sure what to say," she mumbled, tears burning the backs of her eyes.

"Say you'll be my mate." Aldonas slid the tip of his wing under her chin and tilted it up, forcing her to stare into his unnerving yellow eyes. "The sun will set soon, and we'll miss our chance to satisfy Jack Valentine."

Dither's knees trembled; she wobbled on the spot. "But you don't even *believe* in Jack Valentine!"

"I believe in *you*, Dither. From now on, whatever is important to you is important to me." He slid a copper lock into Dither's hand.

"But—" Dither's head was spinning, and the sun was falling fast. "I thought you couldn't stand me. You were always avoiding me and telling me to leave you alone. How can I believe this isn't another one of your games?"

Aldonas held her firmly in his massive wings. "I'm so sorry, Dither. I *have* been trying to avoid you, but I wasn't playing games. Being near you stirred a primal hunger I thought I couldn't control. I pushed you away because I wanted you *so* much. I was afraid I was going to disembowel and eat you."

"Oh? Is that all?" Dither laughed and wiped her nose with the back of her satin sleeve.

Aldonas lifted her off the ground and pressed her into the warmth of his chest. "Dither," he cooed in her ear, "I have never, in all my life, met a more tempting woman than you."

Dither squirmed in his arms until Aldonas set her gently back down. "But what about Elisabetta?"

"She's certainly a beauty," Aldonas said. "You have very good taste in women . . ."

"But?"

"But the lock and key bonding can only work for a true love match, and I'm in love with someone else." Aldonas slid his wing into his pocket and produced the key. "Dither, will you join me in the pleasure pit? Will you help me satisfy Jack Valentine?"

Dither ran a finger over the smooth edges of the copper lock.

"You're . . . *in love*?" Dither asked.

"I think I have been for a very long time," Aldonas said gently, "but I was too scared to know my own heart. I wasn't being honest with myself."

Dither looked from the lock, suddenly very heavy in her hand, to Aldonas' key. "Once we enter the pleasure pit . . ." she said, "that is, if we make a promise to Jack Valentine . . . if you open this lock, there's no going back. We'll be bonded forever."

"Dither, I love you!" Aldonas squawked. "Let's start forever right now!"

"Aldonas, I . . . " A wicked smile spread across Dither's face. "I want you to chase me!" she squeaked, rushing past him into the pleasure pit, threading between groups of revelers in various states of undress, and heading for a pile of overstuffed red cushions in the center of the tent, directly under its opening. She leaped over a human man pounding a pregnant orc from behind, ran past an undulating pile of tieflings, and practically tripped over a cyclops being pegged by a lizardwoman.

The sounds and smells of pleasure were everywhere. Dither even spied Hardwin the manticore with his face buried between a pair of shapely, pale legs. Still, she ran, her focus on the pile of pillows — a proper goblin nest for a proper goblin mating.

Dither could feel her strix hot on her heels. She ran right past one of Arlynn's "no running" signs and into a slick patch of mud, skittering out of control and sliding into the sculpted backside of a siren. Before she could apologize, something soft and heavy and warm knocked her off her feet and pinned her to the satin nest.

Dither struggled and squirmed. She managed to roll halfway over and look up into Aldonas' crazed face. His eyes were huge, burning yellow orbs; his beak was elongated and razor-sharp;

his feathers were blood red. He held her ferociously, gripping her tiny body with talons as long as her forearm. Even in his altered form, Aldonas screeched out three words in common tongue.

"Beeeeee . . . . . myyyyyyyy . . . . maaaaaaate."

Dither gripped the lock in her lithe fingers and stretched it out, presenting its hole for him to enter.

Aldonas held the troll key between the tips of his feathers. He jammed it into Dither's lock and turned. The shackle sprang free, and Dither threw her head back and screeched.

"Schriiiihck!"

The strix word for "I love you," loud and clear, exactly the way Aldonas had taught her.

"Schriiihck!" Aldonas answered. He sank the tip of his beak into her shoulder, breaking the delicate, green skin. Dither's sex quivered when she felt warm blood dribble out of her, only to be lapped up by Aldonas immediately.

"Schriiihck!" Dither called again, tearing at his britches, desperate to free his copper cock, to feel its cold, hard length filling her again.

Aldonas pulled his beak away from her flesh just long enough to bray his devotion.

"Schriiihck!" Dither called. He was hers, finally, after so many years of longing, after giving up on him ever loving her back. Aldonas the strix was claiming her in full view of hundreds of naked Th'myskôrians. Her cunt pulsed and slicked in anticipation of their sacred union.

"I need you, Dither," Aldonas hissed in her ear. "Get my cock ready, please." He rocked back onto a cushion, and Dither pounced on his gleaming dick. She held the singing rod in her nimble fingers and felt the vibration coursing up her arms and through her entire body, leaving a trail of aching need in its wake. She struck it hard with her curved sex rock before pressing her full lips to the tip, claiming with a kiss the shiniest cock in the Three Realms for all time. Dither parted her lips and slid her tongue across its smooth, hard surface, savoring the bitter taste. She groaned as a sharp, metallic zing seared her mouth.

Aldonas bucked under her. "Now! Screeeeeeee! Please!"

Dither slid her mouth down his cock, tightening her lips around the buzzing shaft. His metal dick was cold and hard against her palate, but Dither worked her soft tongue along his length, earning a series of appreciative clicks and chitters. With every sound he made, Dither's excitement grew, and desire was leaking out of her cunt as she worked her mouth down to the feathery base of his cock.

"That's enough!" Aldonas rasped. "Lay back for me."

Dither did as she was told. As soon as her head hit the plush satin cushion beneath her, Aldonas thrust his head under her skirts, burrowing through the fabric toward her eager cunt. He hooked his beak around the waistband of her smallclothes and pulled them down gently. Rough cotton scraped over her legs, then her mate's massive, feathery head.

Dither pulled up her skirts, exposing her sex and clearing his path.

Aldonas pulled off his tunic. He spread his wings, presenting himself to her in all his terrible, beautiful glory.

"You're naked," Dither teased, putting a hand up to her mouth.

"I have a permit," he said, pressing the hollow, bulbous tip of his dick to her slick opening. Dither sucked in a sharp breath. Her pleasure was exquisite.

Aldonas worked his copper cock into her, rocking back and forth on his knees. Its song changed, matching the intensity and the beauty of the orgasm mounting in Dither's core, threatening to destroy her.

"Hold on to me," Aldonas instructed, "tightly." He was still pumping inside of her, stretching her pussy, burying his cock a little deeper with each thrust.

Dither moaned. Her arms were weak, but she wrapped them around his gigantic torso, gripping his soft feathers. She clamped her legs around his hips as securely as she could.

"Do you have a good grip?" he asked.

Dither could only whimper and nod in response — the musical pleasure emanating from his cock was the most intense she'd ever felt. And yet, no force in the Three Realms could have wrenched him from her.

"Good!" In one fluid motion, Aldonas slammed his vibrating cock fully inside. With each merciless thrust, he flapped his massive wings, lifting them both off the ground. Dither squeezed her eyes shut, bracing against ecstasy as every muscle in her body tightened and clenched.

She felt lightheaded. Her pleasure was mounting. Aldonas moved inside of her, pumping his musical cock into her tender, pillowy flesh. All the while, he kept beating his mighty wings, and with every thrust of his cock, the pair rose higher and higher into the air.

Coiled pleasure churned and tugged at Dither's core. As the couple rose above the other revelers — climbing through the air and past the opening in the pleasure pit's tent, soaring above the feast — she shattered. Release thrilled through every part of her body as she arched and convulsed around her strix. Her moans of pleasure were enhanced, controlled by the vibrating of his cock against the inner walls of her cunt.

When she opened her eyes, Dither saw the whole of Th'myskôra shrinking into a blur of lights beneath them as Aldonas carried her higher into the sky. His powerful wings flapped in time with his thrusts, streaking her vision with black and red. Her delicate, shimmering pink dress fluttered around them as Dither and Aldonas twirled and spun through the glistening, misting rain.

When she opened her mouth to shriek that beautiful strix word — the perfect sound to represent the pleasure and pain of being taken, of being marked by Aldonas — a beautiful, multi-colored light poured out of her mouth. It was the light of their bonding.

Dither could feel every cell in her body attuning to him. They were a bonded pair now, joined by the magic of Jack Valentine and ready to spend the rest of their lives together.

"Schriiihck!"

Aldonas threw back his head and declared one final ecstatic shriek, cumming thick, glittering ropes and filling her with his devotion. Dither saw the blindingly beautiful light of bonding stream out of his beak.

As their shared climax ebbed, they floated gently down to the top of a nearby tree where Aldonas nestled on a sturdy branch. Dither finally loosened her grip, snuggling into her strix's soft, warm feathers.

"Now that we're bonded," Aldonas murmured, caressing her trembling body, "where will we live?"

"I don't think I'm a good match for Academy housing," said Dither thoughtfully. "And you'll never be allowed in the Eldrich Forest."

"You could build a new den!" said Aldonas. "We could build one together! Not in a stump, but in a living tree, like this one."

"I love it!" Dither squeaked. "I'll build a traditional den in the trunk, and you can have a nest in the tree top. We'll meet in the middle!"

"Just like grandmother would have wanted," Aldonas cooed.

"A perfect, soft goblin nest," Dither murmured as she snuggled into the warmth of his feathers and they both drifted off to sleep.

THE SIREN'S PACT

Sign up for Mona's newsletter at and get a free copy of "The Siren's Pact".

Set one hundred years in the past. As war looms, Jumana must decide if her loyalties lie with humanity...or with her heart.

ALSO BY MONA HOWELL

The Human Bet

The Forbidden Incubus

ACKNOWLEDGMENTS

I would like to extend my most heartfelt thanks to my wonderful husband. And to by beta readers MC Newstead, and Audrey Ruff. And, of course, to the members of the Princess Cafe.

About the Author

Mona Howell is just a forty-year-old girl writing silly-fun books for the monster smut girlies.